THE DIAMOND ASSASSIN

Fame presents

THE DIAMOND ASSASSIN

THE DIAMOND ASSASSIN First Edition, Jan. 15
This renowned fiction novel promotes change, retribution, and due-process by the founder of Knemiziz Entertainment.

Book cover design & layout by
Inmark design

Quintell
(901) 308-4994

THE DIAMOND ASSASSIN

By F A M E
   O L Y N
   R L   E
   G   M
   I   I
   V   E
   E   S

SHOUTOUTS

I extend a shout-out to every mother and child who rides the never-ending train of poverty and lack of love. I also extend my gratitude to those unyielding motivational people who have stood on the battlefield with me through my days of wonder and hardship, serving time throughout these dismal-crips where slaves are made for these times and Kings are born; furthermore, given homage to all those who stood strong by the code in those Federal court systems without parakeeting, singing like a bird, whistling Dixie, or whatever spin they put on it. It's SNITCHIN at the end of the day, Hommie!!!

On that note, shout-out to the ones who kept it solid and RAT-FREE!!

With all that being said, my family, remember when the allegiance of men has been forsaken, it is one's fate which lies in the hands of Karma....

Extended shout-outs to the big Hommies from the Lou. Nelly / Dirty ENT., Just Bleezy, & the All Stars, Reek from ATL/Black Jewels Entertainment, Pimp Hard, D. Wells, J.T., Fat Charles, Big SKrilla, Derric Smith, Courtney Jr., Sir Tankee Luciana, Mardigrameech, Anthony, Tracy, Sandra, Eva, Cynthis, Cisco and Double R.

Direct correspondence with Author:
Courtney Smith 31022044#
FPC
P.O. Box 2000
Millington, TN 38038-2000

LOVE ONES & HOOD LEGENDS

Shoutouts to COOK AVE:

Peachis, Chub, Moo Moo, Atlanta, Teionna, Cavorrion, Ron Ron, Zayion, Ronnie, Lamont, Cynthia, Jordan, Nay Nay, Baby Doll, Cookie, Ron Love, Kiya, Samon, Nicloe, Amy, Donnie, Jean aka Tuddy, Joice, Monica, Tasha, Punkin, Paula, Eddie, Idella, Duchess, Janariah, Dallion, Lexsy, Robin, Star, Dyna Deal, Lantz Nave, Smoke Dog & wife Tonie, Stuffy, Leonna, Big Snatcha, Wild Bill, Tooie, Keal, Boo Skello, G'Sta, Hucky, Baby Sista, Boo Boo & RIP his Son, Big Noon, Too Tall, Palo & Dimples, Mumbles, Hozay, Scrapy Loc, Jackie Boy, Slick, RIP LIl' Tom, LIl' Tony, Lil' RayMOnd, Lightskin Keysiha, LIl' Wayne, Amp Dog, Steve, Sharee, C-Swift, Bell , Black Chris, Angie, Eddie, Buchie, Carl, Half Head, Randy Ray, Sweepy, Lafar, RIP LIl' Donnal, RIP Rich Loc, RIP Poochie, Wonnie, Mistreaty, Black Mark, Tabud, Kennetria, Rapheal, Bree Bree, Soni, Kim, NIta, Armoni, Ashley, Lonna, Iva, Barbie Ann, Pookie & Jermain, Lil' Girl, Honey James, Moma & Baby, Jamie, Jean Smith, Karmen & Pat, Dontrell, Janeen, Fred & Montrey, Skeet & Woods, Bow, Ray Ray, Antwan Skyes, Bridget, Tonya, Eva Skyes, Ralph, Carrolyn, Dian, Idella Hollis, Alleace Reason, Ingrid, Jennifer Carter, Janet Kennedy, Chiqvita Pope, Larhonda, Big Will, Poona, Nette & Ressy, Coach, JOe from East St. Louis. Joe Womack, Raymond Shoemaker, Earl Smith, Re

Furlough aka (Juneg), Tazz, Pimp Hard, Kevin Tolbert, DeAndre Tubbs, Tut, KD, Lucus, Michael Roggers, John McKinney, B. Rainwaerks, Tony, Big Hawk, Freaky Jun, Chuck, Christa, Dorris, B Girl, Germain & Lil's Ralpheal, Eric Thomas, Big Sip, Big Sed, Mississippi aka T. Holman, Mrs. Brown, Brother Gun, S.S aka Super

Shorty, Shug from Farlen, Fat Mike, Mommy, Big Mike, Shanetta Goodson, Latungerla Bovan, Bonitta Johson, Choo Choo, Lan Lan, Wyane & Dawyane, Vinnie Casico, Ang.

Dimmie & Poah Bear, Lil' Trig, Amanda, Antonio Mitchell (Tony), Charles Cawv Thao, John Nease, Angel & Peachis, Travis & Sweets, BA, Anthony Coop, Fish, Amanda,' May-May, Lil' Yolonda, Ressy, Evett, Latonya & Bey Bey, Randie, D. Butler, Fella, Big Stonnie, Clifton Pierce, Darren Atkinson, Blue Joe-Day, D-B & Meeka, Kenneth Smith, K-Rob, Sincer, 3-9 Reggie Jones, Moe-Moe, Buchy, Carl, Halfhead, Keith, Merry, 4-Loc, Val-val, Ann, Angie, Rip Mike & Sean Meeks, C-Swift Jackie Boy, Detrick, RIP Fat Man, Mickie, Skeet, Woods, Cookie, Shayla, Elv, Ledella, Lil' Tony, Jun-Bug, Fat Charles, Sweeky, Big, Dirty-Red, Tammy & Peewee, Spencer, Ms. Betty Rambo, Jake, Sleepy, Naisha, Rip Lil' Jemmy, James Omar Morris, Tubs, W. Carter, P. Rainey, Danitta, McCall, Mr. Piggie, Charles Peoples aka Lil' Bruh!, Terry Fuller, The Queen Maywest.

Special Shout-out to all those riding the cause in St. Louis Ferguson County for the Big Hommie, RIP Michael Brown, Hands Up, Don't Shoot!

SHOUTOUT TO MY SOUTHSIDE MOB:

Sheen, J-Loc, Uddy, No Trace, Cynthia Yette, Scan Loc, YZ, Bean Pole, Crazy Loc, LD,

Smokie, Insane, Shakeama, Geno Grape, Doug, Shameeka, Quetta, Shay, Tarowbie & dre,

RIP LiP Kenny, Big Money, Big Mike, White Boy Rob, White Boy Ronnie, Glock, RIP J-Rock, Yummy, Sweets, Sharran, Tiffany, Erica, Sheila aka Red, Latrese aka Margo, Jessica, Shagratta, Marlene, Tiny, Foo, Ree Ree, Stacy, Audrey Smith, Molinda Scott aka Boss Lady-Ms Pink, Chrystal,

Chassity & Candice, Tammy, Yo-Yo, Snow, Big D, Willie Berry, Uncle Michael, Bessie, J-Dub, Michael Elliott, Reggie Brown, Calvin Brown, Flossy & Lisa Brown, Amy Adams, Tonette Garrison, Sylvia Keys, RIP T-L.O.C, Keshon, Kaliyah, Jeffrey Rush, Roosevelt (ToeJoe), Bart Stove, Norkita ♡

ADELAIDE: Jus Bleezy.Bull, Booty, Third Kill, RIP Scary Terry, RIP Vick

COLLAGE-N-CARTER: Black, RIP Dre, Stink, Sisco, Da-Zone 20 Street, White Boy, Mark Cherry, Big Skyie, Boobie, VIP Spud, Lil' Larry, Lil' Calvin, John John, Mike Lewis, Kevin Cherry (KC),

44-BUD: Fat Mike, Spiderman, No Brains, Big Enzy

MAFFET: PJ Paul Drake

ALICE & WARNE: Fine, La-Dale, Fattz, Tyrone, Bateman, RIP Big Zac & Lil' Zac, Lee,

GARFIELD: Razz-J, Ranee & Sally **D.S.T:** Rat, Wild Child, RIP Big Pookie

3940 BLOCK OF KENNEDY: K-Fool, Charlie Mack, Row, RIP Loddie Mann, Mz Monk **LABADIE:** Lil' Scrappy, Day Day, Lil' Syke, Big Syke

AND SHOUTOUT TO EVERYONE FROM THE "PAC", AT THE BOATHOUSE. FROM THE NORTHSIDE, O'FALLEN PARK

D.T.: Allen East aka Face, Big Jodie

THE VONS PROJECTS: Diego, Jay, G-Nut, Monica aka Ms Hollywood, RIP Gue, Dee, RIP SK

VERNON aka V.C.: Corleon, Black Mark, Ears, Big Lou, Lonell Cartez, Jason **ARLINGTON MOB:** Pinhead, Reece, Bo, Tone, Meko, Torlon,

EAST GATE: Ali, City Spud, Murphy Lee, Nelly, Fat-E, & Wife Treece, Process **NORTH MARKET MOB:** White-Side, Duce Tone, Sylvester Clay, ETC,

HODIAMONT TRACKS: Fat Ronnie, Static Loc, EP, Big Jodie, KK **WESTSIDE DIVAS:** Marilyn, Torran, Danielle, Chrissy, Tiffany

BEAN STREET: Red Rag, Lil' Allen, X-Man, Tywon, Fonzo, Wonita & Bonita Brown, Brenda, Jo-Jo, Darlene

GRAPE HILL: Pruitt El, Tank, RIP Tawana & Sherrie

THE HORSESHOE: Killa, Paul

BOD**: Rainbow, Dorsey, CoCo, James Brown, Dice, Black Rob, Lil' Chester Goodson

PINE LAWN: Michael Capelton, E Smith, Kevin Knowles, RIP Shaun Holmes

CALIFORNIA LOVE: RIP Tookie, Monsta Loc, Bizz, Tonto, Big Trig, LA

HILLSDALE: Kent

52/54 ROBIN & WREN: Ron, RIP Lil' Darren, CoCo, Stink, Bam, Fat Chris, Ray Ray, Ruben, Patrick ELL, Doobie, Lil' Boone, Monkey Rel, Wordell, Pookie, Lil' Landy, Kevin,

Tony & Will, Valencia, Teddy, Lil' Kitchen, Lil' Mann, Chingy

MAD LOVE FOR THE HOMIE Q REP'N THE NEW YORK 800 BRONX 4-LIFE

SHOUTOUT TO ALL THE LADIES REP'N THE SAINT LOUIS TWERK TEAM AND WHIRL GIRLS

SHOUTOUT TO ALL THOSE REP'N: QUEENS, HARLEM, JERSEY AND BROOKLYN

CHICAGO BROTHERS: Big Mafia, Head, Crusher, Dino, Shake Billa El, Geno, Biz

27 MAC: MD, Smooth, A-Mac

KENT LOCK: Big V, Steve Vaughn, Joe Morris, Tommy & Pat, Wanda

SPIRITUAL BROTHERS: Mr Payne, Mondo, John X from Naptown, Temple #1, Jerry Louis- Bey, G Hosppskin-Bey, Noble Bennett Rush-Bey Brothers

LACLEAD TOWN: Thunder Cat's

MUST HAVE SERVICES

KING STATUS ENT. www.kinglish.com

BEST PHOTOGRAPHER: King Yella',

CREATIVE THINKING MEDIA: DEMETRIUS NEAL

MIXOLOGIST: DJ Cuddy

THE BEST FOOD IN TOWN: Sweet & Savory Catering by Nikki (314) 795-2796

ACKNOWLEDGMENTS

To those whose path I've crossed, that sadly pondered the loss of a love one through any such form of hardship as those in this fictional text. My beloved family of urban; I send my most profound empathy and respect. I also send acknowledgment to **Ms. Diamond E. Mitchell** aka **Young Paula,** who's character within this story has inspired me to reach out to women of all ethnicity.

Souly it has been granularly painful to maintain a sense of humility as I walked amongst the shadows of her life, sadly gazing upon the sprawling depths of a tainted young woman's titanic past pain. To all likewise, may God bless your future affairs with peace, just as he have given me the ability to share many testimonies through the power of storytelling.

As the once lived great warrior INK-KEY-DINK once said,

"Break bread with those you love, for all that envy you, will soon parish before their own hate!!"

CHAPTER ONE – Taken Young

Hustle City lies un-rested in the heart of the *Show-Me* state; where one of America's most wanted crime watches was posted. Stricken by a horrible drunken accident on their honeymoon, were Monica Davis and her twenty year old husband Zac. As it turned out Monica may as well have been sentenced to an early death. A few minutes after the young couple left the Black & Yellow Super Bowl bash in Tampa, Florida wasted. Her husband, Zac, hardly held his drunken balance. His caring father was the designated driver. Staring at his only son from the rear view and not the road as he should have been; the black 1992 Suburban S.U.V. flipped and rolled nearly half a mile before ejecting both driver and passenger through the windshield, leaving the European couple survived by their son Zac and his wife Monica. They were airlifted to the nearest trauma center where Monica underwent several life saving surgeries. As a result, she was diagnosed infertile and her dream of having children died that night along with Zac's parents in the deadly accident.

Several years later, on July 4, 2001, a merciless Caucasian couple pretending to be tourists, not an easy task amongst an ocean of African Americans, but they passed, like magic, through the crowd of naive youngsters.

Open tents were lined up under the legendary St. Louis Arch and bustling with holiday activity. Jam-packed business stands and other vendors were also lined up in their colorful booths displaying their services and merchandise selling them with much savvy mimicking of the high-end vendors of Chinatown in New York City. Rejoiceful children were in abundance representing all ethnic peoples in chuckling, carefree, groups.

The fourth of July V.P. Fair supplied enormous amount of entertainment for children and adults, from amusement park rides, to cotton candy and Fairy Kiya's stuffed animations.

Parents watched expectantly as the fireworks were set to begin.

Chilled in goose bumps, Zac wore a pair of blue slacks, a white button down shirt and white sneakers. He stood six foot tall, but was humiliated by his pale, figureless 200 pounds of blob. He had lost most of his hair since the accident and he felt like a young man trapped in an old man's body which he knew his wife hated to be on top of her. His baldness was a hereditary thing for all he knew, so to sway people, he smiled and dressed like a politician.

Dig that!!

His frost bitten eyes glanced over to his soul companion, Monica. She was a true gem. Brisk winds ruffled her silky auburn straight hair. She stood 5' 6" tall in her expensive BB heels and was attentive to her vicious husband's cold stare. She placed her matching BB designer sunglasses gently over her beautiful light olive tan face. She wore a sly smile that would melt Mr. Playboy himself; sucking the living life out of him.

Monica's artificial smile was to die for. She had used it before to accomplish her ends. It was a well kept secret, she was a genius and a true con-artist. Her eyes swept through the crowd of scattering children, picking over them as if she were perusing a football ticket. As the daylight dwindled, the temperature fell from 90 degrees to a cool 73 degrees with a breeze sweeping St,, Louis' murky Mississippi

River. The city's pigeons swarmed the air above, preparing to roost.

That day marked the anniversary Zac and his wife Monica planned to kidnap an African American girl. Since their accident, the couple had been responsible for the abduction and murder of countless Amber alerts nationwide, ranging from ages six to nine.

Due to it being the couple was upper class Caucasian Harvard graduates, no one suspected them of such crimes. So they counted on traveling the globe, basking in their twisted and treacherous epilogue. It had always been Zac's inner demon that thirsted for the souls of such innocent youth. He'd always chosen their victims. Therefore, he hunted on this particular day without any preference of color.

His ocean blue eyes were trained for child hunting. They led his instincts toward the muddy riverfront as the festive lights shadowed him as the dawning of darkness settled in; which meant more fun for the children. The fireworks were about to cover the entire landing.

"Huh!" he thought. "Now what do we have here? Two girls in their early teens!"

They were much darker and older than he preferred. However, the thought of having them as sex slaves burned inside him!

The girls walked barefooted along the river, tight roping the flood wall in fun. They both were absolutely stunning to him. The sound of the screaming children filled the air with delight. The huge Ferris wheel in the distance continued to spin and the loud music from the calliope screamed with excitement while the children yelled at the top of their lungs with the pure joy of being alive and young and out on the town.

Zac glanced around and noticed a mixed complexioned woman leaning against a gray Volvo while eating a hot dog, obviously attentive to the two girls in Zac's sights.

Zac quickly moved towards the naive mother. "I want them!" he whispered softly.

A short: distance away Monica's green eyes also stared at the woman, then over and questionably back into her husband's icy cold blue eyes.

"Black girls, honey? Come on! You got to be kidding me!" Her lips quickly moved to say.

He nodded yes. Then said, coming up to her, "I'll handle her, you hurry over to nab the girls; and meet me back at the van!" he ordered lowly. "We'll use code seven on this one."

Monica stood facing the swirling, shifting, dark Mississippi River.

Zac moved like a snake towards the van.

Monica stood back a moderate distance pretending to be throwing rocks into the river just as the girls were.

They acknowledged her with friendly smiles. The van pulled alongside the Volvo. The large vehicle shadowed the smaller sports car.

Zac expertly blocked the view of any oncoming traffic. He quickly made his move!

"Excuse me," he said, exiting the van. "Could you tell me where I can find the Adams Mark Hotel?"

"Sure!!" the courteous woman responded with an inviting glow. "It's ah," she attempted to say it before she collapsed to the asphalt, feeling lightheaded. She blinked before she passed out. Zac quickly stuffed the taser back into his pants and covered it with the tail of his shirt.

The young girls were so engrossed in their play, competing to see who'd make the largest splash they never once turned in their mother's direction.

Monica bided her time wisely. The moment she saw the mother crumble, she waved for their attention. She rushed toward the girls until she was short of breath. Her heart and lungs throbbed and burned simultaneously as she began her evil roll.

Action she thought. Then said in a frantic tone, "Come! Come quickly! Your mother has passed out!!"

The girl's eyes widened at once.

"My husband and I are rushing her to the hospital! Hurry!"

The girl's heads simultaneously twisted toward the running van. The sliding door was open. In a flash, they recognized their mother's Princess Reeboks hanging from the van's door. Their eyes locked onto the butterfly and flower tat scaling their mother's right ankle. Without further question, they jumped into the strange van.

The huge Caucasian male aggressively slid the door closed. The woman climbed behind the wheel and ignited the engine as the man overpowered the frail youngsters, binding and gagging them easily after covering their faces with the white hanky soaked with Chloroform.

The door opened and the unconscious woman was gently laid on the ground beside her vehicle. The van's dark license plates disappeared into the July evening.

Monica cautiously drove the van through a maze of tourists and local law enforcement who cleared a path for the van to pass safely. She signaled to merge right onto Highway 70, west.

Moments later an agonizing wall of people began to gather around the troubled mother, who was coming to her feet. When she noticed her children were not with her, she began to scream until a large crowd formed. Sirens quickly blazed in the distance!

In less than an hour an Amber alert was sent throughout Metro St. Louis and the surrounding Illinois areas. The alert went as follows: "A special Amber Alert to the surrounding areas; two ten year old, identical twins, Central West-End, African American girls, Paula Kennitra Roberts, aged 10, approximately 4 feet 6 inches - 75 pounds, and Carla Pauletta Roberts, 10, approximately 4 feet 7 inches tall and 75 pounds, were abducted at approximately 8:32 P.M. from the downtown St. Louis metro area... If you see girls matching this description, please contact authorities at 555-4042...

CHAPTER TWO – Breaking Point

Zac and Monica arrived at their home in Universal City in less than thirty minutes as planned. The suburban, single family home was located in the first county outside the St. Louis city limits. The SUV pulled into the garage, which was awaiting their arrival, when the door was opened all the way by the automatic opener and was fully up.

A welcome breath of '*job well done*' entered Zac's lungs as he stepped from the van stretching his hairy arms and smiling with anticipation of the nights to come.

As he and Monica had aged following the accident, the abductions had become more complicated, and thus, more risky for them. However, Zac was pleased that: they had successfully pulled off another one. He removed the bound girls one at a time and carried them through the door and into the house. He moved quickly, laying their crying, stiff with terror, bodies gently onto the bedroom carpet. There was no need to damage them prematurely he reasoned to himself. He locked the door behind him as he exited the room, smiling with satisfaction. It was cold in the room, but he knew the girls would be fine - for now.

◆

The sun set low in the western sky, leaving a purplish orange wave across the horizon. The only sounds heard in the quiet neighborhood were the sounds of crickets chirping and the soft hum of the residents air-conditioning units. In the distance, the sounds of traffic wafted over the muddy river.

Inside the house, the poisonous and illicit, methamphetamine stimulated couple began their perverted games which they played with their innocent victims.

Since Monica had been rendered infertile and could never bear children of her own, she took her pain out on their innocent captives. Somewhere in Zac's demented brain the conclusion was reached that children were simply objects to be toyed with and later destroyed at his leisure. He kept his secrets well hidden from Monica, whom he knew would not approve of his final acts upon their victims.

"If we can't have our own, why should others?" Zac once told his conniving bitch of a wife. She had seemed to agree with his assessment.

"Shh! Don't cry, Carlie. Mommy will come. I'm not going to let them hurt us!" Paula her younger sister, by four minutes, lowering her voice to a mere whisper as the frightened twin sister leaned closer to her chest. Paula knew they were trapped inside the Gates of Hell which were designed to keep people in once they entered. The windows were lined with steel plates and a Viper alarm system. No child had ever escaped one of their Houses of Pain, as Zac considered them. The girls were forced to wear black and brown magnet school uniforms with matching Cottage Bro shoes during the day as if they were attending school.

The woman produced an eight millimeter camera and began flicking X- rated shots of them with provocative objects as props. Afterwards, the mad couple made the innocent girls perform sex acts

8

on Zac. Paula would take her sister's turn. "Let's just do whatever the crazy's want, until we get away!" Paula warned her sister.

Carla nodded yes. Still the brave girl was just as afraid and worried about her sister, though Carla hadn't been speaking much. She cried out her voice until it pained her to even drink the juices Paula forced her to drink. Paula had no idea Zac's cruddy ass fondled Carla during her previous bath.

Every time Paula spoke, Carla cried like a big baby! She never minded strategizing or attempting to figure a way out. She'd simply withdrawn becoming daunted.

Paula on the other hand, watched everything and listened for any opening out of their perilous situation. Her eyes scanned every single surface, door lock, and outlet in the location, willing to die trying for an escape.

The living room was filled with new furniture - sofas, tables, and glass crystal shelters and plush carpet. The beautiful three bedroom colonial house was purchased by Zac two years prior. It had been almost nine months since their last visit. He loved the walk-in attic and full basement, which served as a great hideout from Monica for his sadistic sexual activities. He would grope, then have sex repeatedly with the victims that his sick mind enjoyed mostly.

The main floor occupied a two story foyer with a sparkling chandelier.

The basement was completely furnished. The couple used their expensive bunk beds. The girls slept together. At night the girls were read bedtime stories and neatly tucked into bed as if they were truly loved. Paula knew something slick was about to jump off. She listened closely as if they were their biological parents.

That night, the girls lay side by side. Carla called her sister by her pet name that only she had used since they were little.

"Ms. Lady, I'm scared!" Carla was more than scared; she was terrified! Carla nicknamed Paula, Ms. Lady after the fact they were left home alone though Paula always talked like an adult telling Carla, "That one day she were going to be someone on TV and that she was going to take care of them for the rest of their lives."

"And don't make me spank that ass!!" Paula would say imitating their mother, Pam, during the hours she was out hustling their next meal. Carla would always giggle so hard, until she cried real tears sometimes. Her giggling days had long past. At this moment Paula could hardly find the words to lighten Carla's fears.

For the sake of their lives, laughter at Zac's corny jokes and pretending to like Monica's bad tasting meals was all the strength they had.

One week later

The St. Louis P.D. found the van stripped in an alleyway of the Metro City. The city wide manhunt for the girls yielded nothing. The investigation had continued and the girl's mom wasn't about to let up on the media's ass about hers! She continued faithfully to storm into the city Justice Center and county substations every morning. The detectives hated to see her feisty ass coming! In a city where crime was as normal as a car thief in Jersey, the police kept their hands full. Officers searched for the girls daily amongst the thousands of others missing nationwide, knowing the two held little priority.

"Ma'am, we've had three 187s within the last 24 hours and we just don't have the manpower right now. Here's my card, please contact me if *you* receive any lead."

The beer-belly caucasian officer pointed her towards the door as he blew his cool breath across his hot cappuccino coffee mug tilting his beady eyes over his wire framed 200 strength reading glasses.

Pam stood totally dumbfounded and disappointed in the St. Louis justice system. Her tax dollars were being wasted on slops like that! How in the world would she hear something before the police?

"All them damn guns and technology they have and you mean to tell me they don't know where my babies are!" She cursed at her friend Sharron as she forked her fingers through her long dark hair. Her eyes sat perfectly under a pair of neatly lined brows that resembled Raven Simone. She let Sharron know that she told those lying ass cops; "The Government could gladly kiss where I'm always wet!" as she stormed from the Justice Center crying a river...

◆

The girls awoke to the smell of fresh bacon and pancakes. Carla ate only a small portion of her cakes. She refused as her sister attempted to stuff them into her mouth. Whenever the woman was distracted, Paula would gobble down Carla's remaining food. She didn't want the couple to consider Carla as trouble. Zac had left on a cigarette errand. The three girls shared breakfast...

"This will all be over in two days!" the woman mumbled aloud as her eyes cornered in tears watching the adorable girls pretended to play as she done the dishes.

Saturday, August 8th was the pretend family's last supper together. They watched the movie, *Shrek Part Three* until bedtime that evening. The man fell asleep on the couch as the movie ended. The woman began taking their empty popcorn bags and cups into the kitchen. Paula noticed a black cell phone had slid from the sleeping man's pocket. It lay crammed between the couch pillows. Paula wasted no time! Her tiny hands moved quickly and kleptomanically. She swiftly pulled the phone out! Zac snored lightly and turned into a more comfortable position, half scaring the girls to death, believing he felt Paula removing the phone! Red wine and all those colorful pills he took all the time consumed him. Paula had no other options, it was now or never for the unique opportunity! Her soft eyes scanned the room for the woman's return. The moon's rays lit through the window onto the sofa where the man lay. Paula's thoughts were to hide the phone.

"Cut if off Miss Lady!" Carla whispered.

Paula pressed the end button and held it 'til the display light went dark. She quickly stuffed it into her Victoria undies just in the nick of time. Monica's long legs entered the room.

"Past you girls bedtime!" Monica said in a motherly voice, as she reached out for their hugs.

Carla's face held a mask of concern.

"Something wrong ladies?" Monica asked with a crooked smile.

"No mommy, her tummy hurts, that's it," Paula lied. She deserved an academy award for the performance that followed.

Monica gave the girls warm, milky cocoa, then put them to bed.

The two girls decided to wait to use the phone. They weren't sure if the couple listened to them at night or not. Paula suggested that they probably did. What the girls didn't know was that the woman sprinkled sleeping powder into their glasses. The powder was Dormin sleeping aid and crushed Seroquel tablets. The girls slept like babies.

Monday, August 9th, about 8:27am, Paula pushed the blanket from over her, using her small feet. Her eyes half open; she reached out to feel for her sister's warmth, something she'd been doing since they were in their mother's womb. Her eyes popped open and she rose to a sitting position. She was alone in the bed! She jumped quickly to her small feet, searching the room! She called Carla's name loud and Monica came running as a caring mother would.

"Shh, it's okay doll!" she assured her. "Banita baby, she awoke early and has only gone downtown with your father."

Paula knew she lied: Carla had always over slept her. The lie silenced Paula and tensed her a bit. It was ninety degrees in St. Louis's county on this Monday morning.

"Can I take a shower Mommy, instead of a bath?" Paula asked.

"I guess so, since your father's not home. It will be a secret just between us girls."

"Yes, ma'am." As Nikki Minji would say, "Paula did it on'na!"

She was taking their fake pretend games and spitting them back into their faces! Monica adjusted Paula's shower temperature and headed to the basement to do laundry.

"Paula, moved fast!" She pulled the lever to turn the shower on then knelt beside the toilet and produced the cell phone. She dialed her mom's cell number. It rang three times before her voice melted away at Paula's heart. Her words hesitated as her young mind bubbled in relief and comfort.

"Hello? Hello!"

"Momma!" Paula whispered, seemingly loud.

"Oh'ma God, Baby! Where are you?"

"Some white people have us!"

"Where, baby?"

"I don't know. They took Carla away. I'm scared mommy, come and get us!"

Pam was also afraid, but more pleased to know her babies were still alive somewhere. She ran around the house getting dressed as they talked. "Ok baby, I want you to look in the trash and find mommy something with the address on it!" Pam screamed as she pulled the drawer open where she armed herself with her ex's nickel plated .40 Glock pistol. She had never touched the gun before. He had left it in her car. Therefore, on that note, she simply kept it for a rainy day such as this. Pam shoved it into her Alexander McQueen bag at the same time tearing the house apart in search of her Volvo keys.

Paula snuck out of the bedroom, tiptoeing into Monica's room. The girl stood at the door and listened quietly. The washing machine still rotated. Paula frighteningly attacked the wastebasket. She thumbed through ripped pieces of paper. It was as if they were expecting her to look through the trash at some point. She spent no time searching the room. She hit the jackpot

"2144 West Pine!" she whispered into the phone "Banita!" The woman began yelling the name she gave Paula. She glanced into the bathroom and noticed the curtain was open as the shower sprinkled vacant of Paula. "Little girl!" she screamed in a panic.

Paula cut the phone off and set it on the nightstand under a tabloid magazine.

Monica began storming through the house screaming at her absence.

"Ma, why are you mad?" Paula wisely pled to her, as she rushed from the room.

"What the hell are you doing in my darn bedroom without my permission?" Monica asked, aggressively snatching Paula by the arm.

"I'm sorry, mommy!" Paula played games with Monica's head. She knew Monica wanted children. Also, that she was weakened by the word mommy. "I wanted to borrow some shampoo," she pled innocently holding a bottle of Pantene Pro-V in her hand. She was on point. Monica apparently believed her but still scanned the room with her penetrating green eyes. She escorted Paula back into the hallway and into the bathroom.

The phone rang and echoed through the house. Monica ran into the bedroom and answered. The man was calling, obviously irate about his cell phone being missing. The woman looked around the room until she found it under the mag.

She answered, "You left it here, silly!" She laughed and they ended the call.

Thirty minutes later, Monica was doing Paula's hair at the time the doorbell sounded. She jumped to her feet in a panic! Sweat poured from Monica' head instantly. The ringing sounded faster and faster! Someone was obviously trying to get in. She hustled Paula into the basement as they had rehearsed.

"We're going to play our little game; hide and seek!" She lied and spoke rather fast. She held the white deep freezer's top open and helped Paula into it. Monica then slammed it and fastened the combination lock.

The deep freezer was empty and unplugged. It sat next to the washing machine. Monica ran up the stairs to the front door. She didn't want whoever it was to draw any attention to the house. Knowing Zac would flip out. She snatched the wood trimmed seven foot glass door open; where she stood face to face with the girls' biological mother. Pam's hair was just as long as Paula's and straight, similar to the girls, brushed over her shoulders. She had the girls' large eyes and black and Indian nose, giving her the best of both heritages mixed.

"May I help you?" Monica asked, her winter green eyes studying the street behind her unexpected visitor.

"Where is my fucking daughters, white bitch?!" the chocolate woman cursed.

"Ah, excuse me! You must have the wrong address, ma'am."

"No, bitch! She called me from this address!" Monica's eyes cornered over her shoulder realizing the clever move the little girl put down before her eyes.

"Not possible," she noted quite girlishly.

Pam was dressed in a black wife beater, red jeans, and no shoes. She placed her manicured palm onto the door as Monica attempted to close it.

"Well, I'm so sorry I couldn't be of any help. Please feel free to try next door," Monica stated with a fake ass grin as she realized there were no police with this firebomb mother that now she envied even more.

She began to close the door in Pam's face again.

"Na'll Ho! You letting me up in 'dis bitch to check for mine!" The olive skin woman rolled her neck.

"It'll be a cold day in hell before I allow you in my home!" said Monica with attitude.

"Fine. I'mma see what the po-lice say!" Pam faked to reach for her phone that she had mistakenly left in her car.

"Shit!" Monica thought.

"Look, I have nosy neighbors. This is a prestigious community. Police calls look tacky! I'll tell you what. If I let you look around, you promise to leave?"

Pam nodded yes. She followed the woman into the house. "Paula, Carla!" she screamed. "Where are my babies?" she asked as she began tearing through the house.

Pam searched the residence with Monica at her heels, pleading all the while, "I told you! Now please leave us alone! And shake up put of my issssh! Monica sassed, emulating black girls.

Pam was looking for anything since she couldn't find her girls presence. She went into the couple's bedroom and searched their hot tub for clues.

She then stormed out. She entered the bathroom in the hall and searched the tub. She leaned down closer.

"Lady, what are you doing?"

Pam ignored the woman and rubbed her index finger across the tub. It was wet. She found what she was looking for. She lifted her fingers and held it to her eye. Her eyes narrowed as she turned to Monica like a snake! Pam smacked Monica and grabbed her by her long blonde hair and dragged her to the bathroom floor, straddling her chest. "Bitch! You and your man on those pictures both have dusty blond hair! Whose black hair is in that tub?!"

Bitch, I swear if you motherfuckers hurt my babies, I'mma kill you dead!"

Pam swore to kill them. She placed her hand into her bag. In the blink of an eye, she held the chrome .40 Glock at the bridge of Monica's thin pointed nose. "Slut, I'mma ask you once more! Where my fuckin' babies!"

"I have her detained!" Monica shouted.

Pam aimed the pistol at Monica's left arm and pulled the trigger.

Paula's heart thumped at the sound of the large caliber blast. All Pam could think about was where were Carla and Paula, knowing they were wondering what was taking their mother so long.

Monica screamed in agony. The bullet entered her soft flesh breaking her collarbone before lodging into the floor. Her blood smeared her hair and Pam's feet.

"Bitch, where is my kids?" Pam asked again. This time Pam pointed her big gun at Monica's face.

Grimacing in pain, Monica replied, "The basement."

"Let's go bitch!" Pam pulled Monica to her feet. She followed the woman towards a door that looked as if it were blended into the wall. Once they entered the huge finished basement, Pam nudged her in the back with the gun. "Hurry up bitch!"

Monica made it to the deep freezer staggering in pain. Pam panicked; she believed they've killed her girls and stuffed them in that box. Her knees weakened. Her heart rate raced. The woman began working the lock's combination. 24 right 32 left and 16 right. Click! The lock snapped open.

Pam shoved Monica's frail frame to the floor and snatched the white top open. Paula was there, lying curled in the box. She was barely conscious.

Pam mumbled in fear.

"Mama!" Paula shouted as she inhaled a huge swallow of air. She was moments from being totally out of air to breathe. She was nauseated as she stood in the small freezer. Pam helped her baby climb out. Paula cried over her mother's shoulder.

"Where is ma other baby?" Pam asked Monica, as Paula's thin arms gladly tightened around her thick waist, squeezing for dear life. Paula's round face stared at the bleeding, distressed woman in hate! Monica's reply was that, "Tawanna were out with her husband for groceries. That the two of them have been gone all morning."

Monica leaned against the washing machine. In tears of remorse and a hurting feeling, she blamed her husband for all these years that had also drove him insane at the thought of his infertile wife wanting to be a mother and unable to. Their pain had driven them to this. She held her wounded arm, staring into Paula's sweet face.

Paula was the only victim that ever played into her sick fantasy by calling her mommy. She realized at that minute, how stupid she'd been played by the little girl she had grown so close to.

Paula rubbed her face, standing at Pam's left thigh, watching the pain eating at the lady's deplorable circumstance of not being able to bear children.

"Sweetie, mommy needs you to be a big girl now. Go upstairs and peep out the front window and let Mommy know if any cars pull into the driveway."

"Okay!" Without missing a beat, Paula nodded and went quickly up the stairs, poking her nose out the silk curtains.

"I swear, white bitch! I'mma put another bullet in you every time I ask you a question and you don't answer, starting now!" Pam cried out deciding it was time to play hard ball. "Now, where is my daughter?!" Pam gritted.

The woman slowly shook her head no.

Pow! Pam's index finger itched. The pistol exploded. A small flame exited the barrel. Monica's heartless body collapsed instantly to the floor.

Her screams echoed through the house.

Pam took a deep breath and stared at the pleading woman in much hate.

The second bullet ripped into her flesh, entering her lower calf, pinning her to the floor.

"Okay! God please, no more!" Monica wanted to live. Her eyes blurred, smearing her vision, as she squinted for words to the determined mother's rage. "I think she's in the wine cellar! Zac said don't go in there!" Monica shouted as she stretched her index finger towards the small door in the rear of the basement.

Pam turned and crossed the huge basement within seconds, dragging Monica with her.

"Carla!" she screamed, as she jerked open the wooden door with force.

They say there's no limit of what a mother will do to protect her young.

Unfortunately for Monica, she had experienced the proof of that!

The small room was dark and musty. It smelled of mold, sewage and something more sinister.

"Carla!" Pam yelled once again, searching the wall for a light switch until her fingers found it. Gruesomely, she wished she'd never cut the tiny light switch on. Her heart shattered in a million pieces the moment her eyes discovered her baby girl there on the floor. She hesitated for a moment.

Pam used the wall to balance her faintful stance. Her legs nearly gave out.

"Carla!" she moaned, her voice breaking with emotion. She dropped her gaze at Carla's tiny body crammed into the dusty corner. Pam gripped at Monica's torn Donna Karren's sleeveless blouse. This bitch was the devil in human cloth, Pam thought as Monica kneeled in submission, torn by the decades of her unforgivable guilt. Globs of blood ran over her silicone breast. She had never indulged in the actual executions of the children. Therefore, as she watched on her wicked mind grieved for the child. Zac had been the one who punished their troublesome children and told his soul mate that the children were always sold off as the government does illegal immigrants.

Pam mustered every last ounce of her strength left in her soul and channeled it to her weak legs to stand.

Due to Pam's haunting cries, Paula suspected the unthinkable had been discovered in that basement. She shriveled into a fetal position between the bed and bedroom window sill. She felt the pain of Oprah during the movie Beloved after losing her daughter. Carla and Paula had been more than sisters. The girls seemed to share twin souls. Paula still held her post on lookout.

"I can't breathe. It hurts like hell!" Monica cried.

"Not her!" Pam said, ignoring Monica's pain and suffering as a bonus well deserved. "Lord, take her!" she sobbed.

In Pam's own way, she would have preferred that it had been Paula instead of Carla. Not that she didn't love them both the same. Carla just weren't as tough as Paula, she was more of a mama's baby and loved people.

"Please not ma fucking ten year old princess! She hasn't even lived yet! Jehovah, you bastard, what the hell wrong with you?!" Pam continued to curse God, staring into Carla's beautiful hazel eyes frozen in pure terror.

The hate in Pam flowed through her tears. From there it traveled up her legs through her torso and filled the top of her head. She used her fingers to close Carla's eyes. She was still as beautiful as ever. She had been stabbed to death.

Pam blinked away her tears. She had done the one thing any mother dreaded most. Her chest ached with grief. It choked her as her fingers examined her daughter's little panties. She lightly ran her fingers against her vagina. She knew instantly that Carla had been molested. Pam became like Micheal, the Angel of Vengeance. Viciously dragging Monica from the small cellar by the roots of her long hair and into the hall where Carla's twin could hear the crucial work she was about to put in on the bitch that murdered her better half! Rage burned through Pam's veins. Her blood began to boil. She skull-dragged Monica's buck-o-five frame near the home movie theatre and shoved her face onto the concrete floor! Monica looked up into the mad woman's brown eyes that favored the girls. She dropped a tear and for the first time in her life, she felt freed from the tormenting results of her terrible accident. She apologized to Pam.

"I'm so sorry. He'll be home soon. Kill that bastard as well!" Monica declared before Pam pulled the trigger until the clip was empty. Then she reloaded and waited . . .

CHAPTER 3 – Coming From Where I'm From

"I'm going down…"

Mary J. Blige

PRESENT DAY 2014

Paula thought the same since she was eleven after burying her 'heart' in that small, beautiful, canary marble casket. Now, since Carla's death, Unfortunately at this day and age of 23, the once sweet girl lay bound and barely conscious in the filth of Blood-Tone's Chevrolet Caprice Classic's trunk. Nothing was new to the hell raising girl after losing her twin and loving mother in such a tragic way, her having been sent to prison for 22 years behind the two homicides. At this point in her life, Paula was getting it how she lived!

"Why do I always find myself in these marvel predicaments?" she asked herself. The funk from the trunk's oily interior caused her stomach to thump and the taste of the fresh blood from her busted bottom lip lingered bitterly.

Tone punched her as if she were a UFC fighter. Her eyes rolled to the top of her skull and she collapsed unconsciously. Unbeknownst to her, she had been lifted from the cold concrete floor and tossed roughly on top of his spare tire and tool box.

The sun beamed high in the eastern sky owing another delightful, low windy morning.

Tone always packed a large *ratchet*. Big Ugly, he had named the .44 magnum. He was known to be handy with the tool shoved in his loose, Young American jeans, covered by a designer jersey he bought at 'Big Y.A.'s East St. Louis fashion boutique. Tone pulled Big Ugly from his hip and placed it under the driver's seat as he pulled up to the South End of East St. Louis, near the John Desheild Projects. He wiped sweat from his forehead. "I can't believe I actually caught this bitch!" he mumbled to himself.

Inside the funky trunk, the sun heating it up so bad, that it began to feel as if Paula was being baked in Big Momma's oven. She felt perspiration beading on her forehead. Blindly, she felt around the trunk's floor for a cloth. It was no secret her smooth talking ass was on a life-long treadmill running out of control since that night she hit Bow and Blood-Tone for all those damn drugs. She spent large and wistfully fast.

Due to Paula's new paranoid behavior toward strangers, she had no friends. She would never trust another with her life as she had with Stinky's snake ass! She became very vindictive since losing her mother and sister. Everyone around her was blamed for her own actions. Paula grew up alone in the downtown Eighth Street projects. Her mother was now serving twenty two years in Chilicothe, a women's prison for double murder, for killing Zac and Monica that had murdered her daughter. Although the community backed Pam, the justice system failed to bend in her favor, for vigilante justice. Being that she killed 'one of theirs', Black America gossiped.

The judge stood firm on his sentencing, beyond the circumstantial evidence of self defense. The biased United States Constitution prohibited revenge. Nevertheless, in one case, seven out of twelve jurors found no guilt in a multimedia case of a mother who had buried her five year old daughter alive, but on the other hand, applauded after Pam's verdict was read.

Pam's childhood mirrored one of many young black girls from the ghetto. A story that spawned through the turmoil of criminal injustice! Pam could never figure out the purpose of the U.S. Constitution. Being that blacks were found guilty, regardless of their findings, prove reasonable doubt in many cases as in her own. Her sentence turned out to be a gift and a curse. She was beginning to learn the truth about this crooked system and how she'd lost all communication with her only loved one – Paula for the first nine months.

Since Paula lacked the immediate family upbringing, she was raised by a Haitian foster family, only for a short period of her teen years, as was her idol, Keyshia Cole. The one thing that was preordained for Paula, and her sad situation which wasn't changing anytime soon, was the fact that she was blessed with Goddess genetics. At the young age of twenty one, she realized that her mother did leave her something you couldn't get at the doctor's office, nor could any prescription sold over the counter complete a woman.

Paula was a born diva; she had no idea, the gift her mother blessed her with. Resembling the stunning C.E.O. of the T.I.M.S. Kidney Foundation, Nicole Pace, light, honey complexion, glistened in the midwestern sun.

On this day, Paula wore navel high cream colored shorts, matching her black and cream bikini top. Her small toes glossed with French tips. Paula was no school girl. There she lay in Tone's trunk, drifting in and out of consciousness. Her mind kept wandering back to that unforgettable day in her past.

PAULA'S DAY DREAM

Two red cardinals joyfully danced a few feet above her boyfriend's cotton candy paint job on his Challenger, on twenty-eights. Paula was reflecting her troubled life as she lay there facing death once again. She was reminded of her ex- Peter's car being Jetty black. It was said to be his pride and joy with Jack Night doors. The Challenger sat stuntastically clean, its candy pigment taking in the St. Louis sun.

Peter had close to eighteen speakers installed, which made his woman deaf, dumb and wet. He was papered up more than most dudes and Paula had his nose wide open. He knew he had the hottest chick in the S.T.L, at his side. Unbeknownst to Paula, behind closed doors, Peter was a totally different person. He was the classic Dr. Jekyll and Mr. Hyde. He was a whacko, or maybe better yet loco!

The first time she noticed his drastic change was the day she caught him in the bathroom pointing a loaded gun in the mirror. "You motherfuckers ah never take me!" he growled.

She had rolled her eyes and left him to the imaginary movie he was making. The next episode was the day he walked into the house and slapped the dog shit out of her and punched her in the mouth. He swore he saw her riding in some nigga's truck! Paula had been home all that day. The third encounter came one winter when Ty, Peter's friend came home from prison. The guys hit the town to celebrate Ty's release. The occasion caused for a lot of drinking, drugs and pole dancing. Fellaz night out, as always.

Ty had never grown used to his manz being tied down by one

28

woman. There's some guys who lead, while others who are born to follow. By no mistake, Tyrone a.k.a. Dink; Peter's childhood rappy was a leader. That night they came from the club pissy drunk and passed out on Peter's living room couch. The following morning Paula remembered being awakened by the sound of a dog fight taking place in her front room. Broken glass, manly cursing and grunts conveyed the drama. She covered her diamond studded eyes and hoped what she was seeing was the boys just rouging around as she entered wearing a see through nightie. Her thoughts were wrong. The boys were wrecking shop. She knew to stay out of it. The men were too strong and wild for her to throw her hands between them.

"What happen?" she asked, surprised by their sudden beef.

Peter regarded her over the rim of his Gucci shades. Unbelievably attractive, her honey colored complexion glowed in the ceiling lights.

Her glossy lips twisted in a frown. She never noticed the bruise over his right eye.

He slipped on his mirror tinted Aviators sun-wear, and produced his forty Glock pistol. Her eyes looked into his. He removed his shades and revealed his blood shot, red devil eyes, which burned holes in Paula's as she stared at him in fear.

"You fucked that nigga while I was asleep last night!" He accused her, mashing his finger in her forehead.

She laughed and he lost all control.

"Bitch! I'mma kill ya' yellow ass, and that nigga!" Peter was crazy. It was final. Her mind was made up! Angry veins popped from his forehead.

"Baby, I'm your bitch! I'll never cross you like that. Pete, you tripping out again!" she pleaded, guarding her face in case he thought to put his hands on her again. "I love you, Pete!" Paula cried out, afraid.

He said nothing. He continued to give her that smack down stare. Unusual, this time Paula didn't blink. He had warned her far too many times that when she blinked, she's lying. He waited to see will she crack.

"She gone crumble before long," he hoped.

It would surely place her there with his boy Dink. Paula wasn't about to fall for the same old banana in the tail pipe trick again. She was one who learned fast. Her being unbreakable caused this bastard to go into a rage. He hit her in the eye with a closed fist! She collapsed to the carpet holding her face tearless, but hysterical.

"I'm gonna ask you one mo' fuckin' time!" he barked. "Did you fuck that nigga?" He stood over her. "And ya' ass bet not sit here and lie to my damn face! Cause when I woke up, I smelled you on him!" Peter had evidently forgot that he and Dink got laid by the twins, Wonita and Banita that night.

"Hell no!" she cursed.

He fingered through his goatee still standing over her crumpled body. He took a pull off his Purple Kush he had in his left hand. "I believe you, beautiful," he stated, taking a long drag from his Kush, turning his nose up exhaling the smoke toward the lights. He then turned and stumbled up the carpeted spiral stairs. Paula noticed that her bedroom had been torn apart. Followed by her clothes being tossed down the stairway, Peter had gone to their room and went ballistic. He called her names repeatedly.

Disoriented, Paula found it hard to see. She reached for the sofa, lifting herself, headed to the back porch to be alone with her tears. The damage inside the house would be left untouched for her to clean.

"God, what I'm going to do? I love this crazy man!" Paula cried. "I'm so afraid to be alone again. How do someone leave all they have?" Tears continued to trickle down her beautiful, bruised face. "He don't look at me the same anymore. He tells me that no one wants me but him and that the next nigga will only use me and make me work the streets." Paula was distraught and confused.

"I wish I would have gone to jail with my mother," she cried out.

It hurt like hell that day when the district attorney decided she was acting under the influences of an adult and spared her of all criminal prosecutions.

"It's so funny how my life turned out over such a short period of time. Lord! Please give a bitch a break!" She looked up to the sky. "Big G, what have I done to deserve such hatred from your mighty hand?" She placed her face in her hands. "I know you said to be patient and your blessing will come, but Lord, only you know I need my blessing right now!" Paula stopped crying and looked up again and smiled. She continued her desperate prayer. "Jehovah God, watch over me and protect me Father. Gotta go. I hear Satan coming, Amen." she closed.

Peter stood before her at the door a whole different man. He acted as the Peter she fell in love with long ago. He extended his hand toward her, smiling like a gentleman. "Why are you sitting out here, baby?" he asked. "Come on, let's go to the show and see, Twelve Yars a Slave." He knew she adored Oprah Winfred act. She smirked as he helped her to her feet. She wondered how a person so young could have such a serious mental disorder so far advanced.

Peter walked her to the car, hand in hand, like the truest lover. It was a reminder of when he was her sweet loving Peter. In her eyes, he was the coolest guy in the world. He did things most guys with money would consider 'tricking on a hoe.'

For instance, he not only forked over money for her expensive shopping spree, online at Dash Clothing, and more, he would sit patiently in a sea of babbling women, waiting for her shoe shopping. Sometimes, Peter would be the only man in the waiting area amongst twenty five partially dressed divas that thought he was a sweet man.

On Paula's nineteenth birthday bash, he made a grand entrance driving a burgundy STL series Cadillac Escalade. Paula saw it parked at the curb in Forest Park, at the new fountain. The engine died and Peter stepped out, wearing a green Polo shirt, a parir of yellow Murder By Design shorts, with a yellow and green Oakland A's baseball cap. Paula loved the way his new addition green and yellow Air Force One sneakers moved dope boy fresh across the well kept grass toward the crunk crowd of mostly divas. Birds chirped high on the parks maple trees. As Paula hugged her man, warm butterflies danced through the spring air. Mosquitoes buzzed around taking bites out of the haters!

They feasted on every stunna exposed in skimpy outfits.

Paula pursed her lips. Her eyes zoomed in on Peter looking larger than life at that moment, she knew she was head over heels infatuated with him. He presented her smile with the keys to her birthday gift and watched his boo scream in delight. Peter had gotten high at that stage. She and her partner Freaky Marolyn ran to the stunning truck and skid away, smiling bumping, (Em'am make it rain on'um!) To her, the SUV drove as if it was floating on smooth waters.

For her, those were the good ole days.

Paula flashed through her life story as Tone accelerated through traffic.

She frowned and stared out the window by the time her and Peter made it to the theatre, her thoughts were hidden. Paula had been putting up with his abuse for four and a half years. Enough was enough. She declared the next time an open opportunity arose she was getting away from his bullshit, once and for all. Had that day finally came? That was a great question for her.

HER FLASHBACK CONTINUED

CHAPTER FOUR – Lonely Prisoner

Paula floated in the empty space of the living room in their three bedroom home located in St. Louis's Wellston County, which is gang infested with two-bit Merchants and Blood gang activities. The house had two Pergo wooded bathrooms and a finished entertainment room that was just painted. Paula figured since Peter kept her hostage in their dwelling, she might as well make him spend on her comfort.

The doorbell rang and Paula glided barefoot and relaxed over her new plush, violet carpet. It felt like heaven between her toes as she wiggled them walking to the door. Making it to the door, she noticed Stinky, her only trustworthy friend, standing there. He was accompanied by two large, white, Wellston Police officers. Stinky looked awful. Nervous as hell, he continued to ring the tiny doorbell as if he were being chased by Freddy Kruger. The officers mugged him and narrowed their gaze.

''Come on sir, no one's home," the blond cop said. "We got to take you in," he added.

Stinky began pounding frantically on the door. Paula deactivated the Brink's alarm system and opened the door. All three men stood as if in a trance, admiring something so beautiful living in such a rundown neighborhood, unnoticed.

Paula took a glance at herself through the reflection of her glass screen door. Now she understood why they were staring. She looked as if she was preparing for Nelly's Tip Drill video.

Stinky's heart plummeted to his gut as Paula toddled her pretty toes in amusement. She stood there looking exotic, displaying her nipple prints. She was taught to always be proud of her Black heritage. Her hair was wet and hung over her shoulders. She wore a half sports bra and Spandex fitted boy-shorts.

"Does he live here, Ma'am?" The man finally asked the magic question.

Paula's eyes darted to Stinky. He gave the diva the puppy look, a classic move from a vet. "Yeah, what did he do, Sir?" she wanted to know.

"We caught him creeping around your property. Plus, he don't have any I.D. on him," the cop replied. "Oh, and you need to get that taken care of, mister!" he added.

"In that case, yep, He lives here. He's my crazy cousin," Paula lied.

The blond officer thanked her for her cooperation, then they ran to their car and sped away, pursuing another gangland shooting.

"Thanks, my dude. That shit was close as a *motherfucker!*" Stinky said, placing his arms around Paula, at the same time complimenting her on her revealing outfit.

She led him into the house, glancing over her shoulder. "Stinky, what the fuck were you doing creeping around my house with your crazy ass?" she demanded. "Ya ass know damn well Peter will kill you if he caught you over here," she growled.

"Man, I know how that nigga is cut! He pulls that crazy shit with you because you a bitch!" He paused. "I mean, a woman."

"Yeah, get that shit right, nigga!" Paula said, sassy.

"Naw, real talk home-girl. That nigga could get it whenever around this bitch!

To be honest wit you Paula, niggas don't even pay that nigga all his change," Stinky explained. "That's probably why he be so mad when he comes through that door and take all his frustration out on you! Yan Ming!"

Paula felt some truth in what Stinky had said. She rolled her eyes to gather the tears forming in the corner of them.

"As a matter of fact, that fool is over on Wobada trapping from Tyreda's spot right as we speak!"

Paula interrupted his spill, "who in the hell is Tyreda?"

"Man, she ain't nobody but a hood bus-down rat! Real talk, that bitch some cold garbage!" Stinky continued, "Her name would never fit in the same sentence as yours."

That comment made Paula smile.

"Why you think I came over here?" Stinky assured her sitting on the couch next to her.

Paula sat back. She longed for some good company. Peter never allowed any visitors ever since the incident with Tyrone. Her and Stinky were high school buddies and have always been partners. She'd never let anyone get too close to her except him. Stinky was the first to persuade her to test drive an X-pill. He looked bad that evening, she thought. His clothes weren't clean and he carried a slight musk odor. Paula wasn't used to seeing him out there like that.

"So what's been up? How you feel being a prisoner in your own spot?" he joked.

Paula dropped her head in shame. Stinky knew because Peter's dawg-ass bragged about it in front of Tyreda's customers. Paula never replied.

Stinky, at once, realized that his sarcasm hurt her feelings this time. It haunted her so much throughout the years of being Peter's maid and sex slave, daydreaming caged up in that damn house without any friends outside of Stinky calling her on occasion. In her own way, she knew how Peter was all along. Hearing it from Stinky though was twice as embarrassing. She knew how Peter drug people's business around town.

Stinky quickly apologized. "I'm sorry. You good?" he asked.

"I'm good," she lied.

Stinky flirted with Paula as usual, touching at her legs playfully.

She laughed. "Stinky, please. Not if you was the last man on earth!"

This struck him deeply. Though he'd been secretly in love with her since high school. To hear her say such hateful words cut him deeply across the heart.

Her living room consisted of a leather sofa, two Lazy-boy chairs facing the wall that held an expensive 60" flat screen Sony plasma HD television. Paula called it the one eyed monster. She hated watching TV. It was all deceptive reality. To her, life was much more than a movie script. When she did make time for it, she watched *The Wendy Williams Show*, or something on *Lifetime For women*. The sofa faced a rectangular table, which Stinky dropped seven capsules and a bag of kush on top of.

"What the hell is that?" Paula inquired with a frown.

"Check it out. Remember the X-pill I gave you?"

"Um, yeah?" she recalled.

"Well I'ma let you try this *new crazy* that everybody is doing! Stinky emptied out one of the capsules on the glass table top and pulled his dingy wallet out of his pocket and removed his ID card.

Paula's eyes widened. "I thought the police said that you didn't have no ID?" she stated strongly.

"Yeah, like I'ma give two rookies my ID and I got two damn warrants on me!" he said laughing. "Paula, please stick to housekeeping."

They enjoyed another soulful laugh. Stinky used the card to separate the powder into several small lines. He produced half of a *Wendy's* straw from his shirt pocket and consumed a deep breath, sniffing back all the excess snot that clogged his burned out nostrils. He leaned over and inserted the straw into his left nostril and inhaled.

Paula watched in amazement as the line of powder disappeared into the *Wendy's* straw. Stinky bounced away from the table as the potent drug traveled through his brain. He mumbled and slumped forward, sitting at the edge of Paula's sofa.

Paula's eyes were glued to him. His eyes were half closed. He sniffed hard.

The drain made the drugs come sliding down his throat. Satisfied, he smiled.

"Go ahead," his voice more mellow now. His body began to relax in a nod.

Paula thought of Peter's slimy ass and hesitated to pick up the deadly straw.

She looked back at Stinky for a second; maybe to check what he was doing.

He was floating like *Elroy Jetson* in another dimension. He stared at nothing with those little black, beady eyes. Stinky wasn't tall, maybe 5'9" at best.

He was so happy for a reason she hardly understood.

Paula inhaled the heroin into the straw fast. It dissolved in her fresh nostrils. She slowly sat the straw back on the table and slouched on the sofa. At first, she felt nothing, as Gladys Knight and the Pips' *Neither One of Us* played from her stereo. Each time she swallowed, there was a thick glob of the drug going down her throat. Her insides tingled. Her eyelids fluttered and the odd effect began. Within seconds, her head grew heavy and her mind moved slower as if gravity increased. It was as if she'd taken a seat on Mars. They did a couple more capsules before she put Stinky out. He left her with three of the capsules and a clear warning. "If Peter finds out, he will kill you, so you better keep it to yourself."

Paula moved in slow motion around the house, feeling light as a feather, cleaning. She suddenly had an urge to hear some different music. Loud music. She went to the stereo and found her favorite diva CD, Lil Boosie and Webbie, featuring Bun B. She played her number one anthem, *Girl Give Me That!* It lifted her mood. The sound of Boosie's voice caused her to hug herself as if she were about to have sex with herself. She put it on repeat and showered. She noticed during the moment she was high, she was carefree. Enough courage to take on the world. Even the mighty Peter was a kitten to her. Later, Paula was seated on her bed in her sexy J.C. hot pink panties and bra, painting her toes by the time Peter arrived home. As he entered their Chanel scented room, he couldn't help but notice her neatly shaved coochie.

"You waiting for me?" he asked, sucking his lips with his tongue.

"Yep, I ran you some bath water."

"Hurry up, Mama got a treat for you!"

Peter nearly broke a leg stripping out of his clothes, rushing to his warm bath. Paula waited until she heard the door close and snorted half of another pill. Her coochie was ocean wet, so wet that thick white gushness leaked down her thighs. Ten minutes later, Peter returned to the bedroom. He heard her softly moaning. He couldn't believe what he was witnessing. She had already drilled that pussy with her toys. He had no idea what she had on deck for him tonight. He was right.

Paula was stretched out on the edge of the bed, fingering her moistness with a pair of burnt orange *Cookie Johnson* stilettos on her feet. Spread wide open, she dug deeper into the carpet.

Peter watched on, thinking, '*she playing in that muthafucka like a violin.*' He'd never seen her in this fashion before.

"Mummm," she moaned and demanded him to hurry up so he could taste her wetness. Paula's eyelids were sealed shut, like a lizard,

'*What done got into you, girl?*' he wondered, moving in for the kill, Peter was rock hard. "What, you popped an X-pill or something?" he questioned her sudden animalistic sex drive. He glanced around the room and spotted a glass of vodka, half empty. She stood as she heard his footsteps. She pushed him aggressively on the bed and jumped into his lap. She reached behind her and inserted the head of his shaft into her ocean of love, with no strain.

Her water was thick, white and wet; super wet. She rode the tip of his love muscle slowly. She wanted him to beg for the rest of her loving. They both burned with a desperate sexual desire. The more he thrust against her wetness, the more it teased him. The longer she rode him, the more vulnerable she became and he noticed. He would ease up for a minute only to hit the right spot each time she lowered her wetness onto his lap. At every point, she felt him pull away. Peter inserted his thumb into her rectum. Paula rode him harder. She was beginning to drive him crazy. She felt the vein on his penis enlarge to its fullness, hitting her lower walls. She unstraddled him and began tasting her own juices from his shaft. It felt as if the tip of him were penetrating the back of her head.

Both of them were at the point of exploding. Paula begged for him to re-enter her wetness. She demanded for him to do surgery with his tongue before she rode him like a stallion, finally they reached their climax.

The drug took Paula to a new high. Peter had never experienced such savagery.

He was literally slobbering at the mouth off her animal lust. She wasn't done yet.

Her pink lips toyed at her own C-cup breast as she grinned at his face. He was great at giving her head. She ground her wetness as deep as she could into his face. Paula wanted him to taste all the nasty semen he squirted in her, along with all the other trifling bitches he'd cheated on her with.

His entire mustache was soaked in her, and his, sticky juices. She was in super nova. She slid down his body like a snake and landed on the carpet. Every inch of her was covered in sweat. Peter still sat slumped at the edge of the bed, waiting for another erection. Paula was still the life of the party. She was now on her knees with her head in his lap, letting her Becky loose, to get him back hard. She held his penis with one hand and gave it therapy, talking to it, and it listened. He began squirming, pulling her head away. Needless to say, she wouldn't let up.

Peter was screaming like a virgin being hit for the first time. Just as they ceased their compelling session she let Peter's penis slump, out of semen.

He was too weak to rise to his feet!

Paula closed her brown eyes as the shower's cold water softly touched her silky skin. *'Damn, that shit felt good!'* she thought, amazed at herself.

The cherry-scented Sex Code body wash dangled from her sensitive nipples.

She was referring to the feeling of the heroin, more than the sex itself. Paula had just become addicted.

CHAPTER FIVE – Tamed

Paula continued to dwell on her past, while still in Tone's trunk. As the old saying goes, 'a young bull and his father were standing on top of a hill. Soon, they came spiraling down at a herd of fine bred heifers. The son looked over at his father and said, "Dad, let's run down and fuck one of them heifers!"

Calmly his father replied, "how about we walk down there and fuck all of them heifers?" Paula must have missed that statement based on Stinky introducing her to that Devil's powder. She had been rushing at full speed into a brick wall. She made Peter go crazy.

Her days of being captive were now long over. Petere still didn't know she had become addicted to heroin, nor did she know that she had gotten someone killed already.

Last Thursday, May 26, about 1:00pm, her and Peter sat in the rear of the Waffle House eating a late brunch. While on the other side of town, Stinky walked into their back door, which Paula had left open for him to take a few electronic items Peter could easily replace. Needless to say, Stinky took more than he was told to. Paula should have known better than to trust a dope fiend. He couldn't help himself. He went straight for their bedroom.

He stole jewelry, a Wii console game, and a 42 inch flat screen TV. He locked the door from the inside and climbed out a basement window. He then forced his way back in the same locked door, making it look as if it were a forced entry.

Paula planned it in detail so Peter would believe it. Peter lost his mind the second he realized his crib had been invaded. He switched instantly into Mr. Hyde and began stalking the house with his Desert Eagle fueling his internal raging fire.

"I'ma blow somebody's fucking head off!" he yelled, then turned to Paula. "Why the fuck the alarm wasn't activated?"

"We walked out at the same damn time, babe! We both forgot!" she rolled her eyes at him, frowning.

Peter got agitated. He stormed out of the house, slamming the door behind him so hard that the table top crumbled into pieces.

Paula called Stinky that night. "I swear I'ma tell that boy on your ass nigga!" "He gone yet?" Stinky asked, whispering.

"Yeah!"

"Open the door then."

Paula let him in the house knowing she shouldn't. He short-handed her on her cut. She was dumbfounded to drug weight.

"Got her ass!" he smirked on the inside. That was the beginning of the end for Paula. Her addiction would become an unsustainable monster. The day after Peter's shit was stolen he was driving Martin Luther King and noticed something that made him bust an illegal U-turn in the middle of the street. He parked on the curb and jumped out of his vehicle, moving swiftly.

"Yo homie! That's my muthafuckin' chain you rockin', my dude!" Peter was mad as hell. "Where the fuck you get that, nigga?"

As Peter walked up, the group of youngsters reached in their waist for whatever they were packing. They were real killers. Each one of them had at least two bodies on count.

"Nigga, you need to bounce before you get ya shit twisted back, fool!" Whiteside said, wearing Peter's chain.

One of the cats dressed in a black hoodie raised his shirt, flashing the handle of his .40 Glock. "You heard the big homie, cuz!" he growled, placing a fist into the palm of his hand, like them fools from Cali do. "Now get somewhere 'fo they find ya ass somewhere, stankie!"

Peter backed away, nodding. He understood their pistol play and had no choice but to respect their gangsta.

About twenty minutes later, a black, tinted out Grand Prix parked at a known spot where the thugs trapped from on the corner of 4201 Pendleton and North Market. Suddenly the Grand Prix amerged, it slid up beside a fine hood diva named Sopheiah. Whiteside and his lil homies were there pulling an all nighter trapping. The black Grand Prix's engine died and both front doors came flying open. A Missouri temporary plate sat in the rear view window. Two men exited carrying street sweepers. Peter and his man opened fire at the crowd of men. Sopheiah, A.K.A. Soso, covered herself beside Whiteside's candy midnight blue old school, sitting on 22's, which represented their gang logo. Bodies began dropping like dominoes when the twelve gauge buck shot pierced their flesh. Duce Tone, attempted to run across the street, but Peter aimed and sent four loud shots at him. Buckshot's entered his back. Only God knew if he'd live or not. Peter ran to the falling man who was rocking his chain.

Soso appeared from behind her baby's father's whip holding a huge 9mm. Her black and orange San Diego fitted cap lay draped backwards over her hair, pulled in a long set it off hairstyle. Her man, Whiteside, sprinted through a cut for his chopper. Soso, violently pointed the business end of her barrel at Peter, blasting at him as if he was from a rival gang that she hated.

Her eyes tightened focus. She ran across the dead grass lot in a pair of Fendi four inch heels as she hunted her prey.

Whiteside trained his son's mother daily, as if he ran a special forces unit, Soso was that chick and the city knew it. She was hot to death and tough as nails. Just like her man, she took no shorts from anyone! It was bang with the hood or find a plot to be buried in.

It was obvious for anyone to see which end she chose. Peter's slimy ass ran like he was playing dodge ball. She wasn't too good of a shot, as she was rolling her ass, but she was handling her business just the same.

Whiteside cared less about her trigger finger, as long as she could shoot cum two feet across the room. Besides, homegirl would bust that hammer at the wind if it blew hard enough. They had called it and Peter soon made it back to his Grand Prix, which was only seconds away from a tasty Chinese restaurant that was crowded with onlookers. He hid among the crowd from the remaining shots directed at him after Whiteside bodied Peter's boy, that had rode with him on that bunk mission over a punk ass chain that barely cost twenty-six hundred. Rose gold at that. Peter needed his ass kicked!

(I GUESS FOR SOME A MATERIAL DEATH WEIGHS MORE

THAN A PHYSICAL LIFE.)

The assault ended as quickly as it started. The crackling of gunfire subsided. Hustle City's night life once again under another full moon. The Grand Prix was last seen flying graciously down Martin Luther King Drive. Only two bodies rocked the city that night.

It was, after all, a good day, or so law enforcement reported. North Market was quiet as kept, however a mere twenty blocks from Peter's home, Paula had begun to slip deeper into the abyss of her habit.

Peter returned home grieving the loss of his partner and chain, without a word about that night being spoken of to Paula. Within months after that day, Peter noticed Paula's sudden mood swings and lump sums of money missing from their petty cash box, which she denied taking.

"Hoe, are you using dope?" he asked one day, agitated at her ever running nose, nods and sniffling during dinner.

"Boy, you tripping. I just be tired," she lied.

He smoked that good purple. Therefore, she knew somethings slipped past him. After all, Paula had forgotten he'd been well into the heroin game long before he met her. On that note, her addition were obvious.

"This broad has been claiming to have a cold for over three months now!" he said to himself, staring at her sleeping.

CHAPTER SIX - Busted

Peter slid word to his boy Kevin Nelly, known as Kelv, who also was currently a high roller in the heroin business on a small block called Adelaide, off of West-Florisent in St. Louis' north city.

On the low he knew Kevin had once lived with an addicted woman as well. Paula's ever running nose stood out the minute his eyes melted over the stunning vicious diva staring at him with a canine mug. Peter wanted to believe anything but the truth.

"You know what that shit is nigga, don't fool yo' self! I know that pussy just good and got chu wide open right now Homie, but you need to see this shit for what it is before that good shit and innocent face be the cause of yo' fuckin' death, fool!" Kelv mentioned.

Peter's head shook in denial. It was sad to see.

"Look here my bud. Uma' keep it hunnit wit' chu. That bitch is long gone and you know it. I know how that dope pussy have a nigga! But still, all in all, the truth can't get no plainer. We both know how this shit gon' end before it gets better."

Kelv kept it gutta and assured Peter by putting his words on their hood.

The 2100 block of Adelaide.

Kelv laughed.

That night Peter devised a plan. Kelv returned at 8:00pm. Had

Paula not been high, she would have known something was foul with the two. Since when did Peter's paranoid ass allow niggas around her so much in one day? They weighed fourteen grams of China White, Kelv had brought over, out of Paula's eyesight.

"Good looking out ma' dude," Peter said, letting Kelv out the front door.

"Paula!" Peter yelled from the dining room towards the kitchen where Paula pretended to clean. She rushed to his voice like a puppy.

"Ba, hide this in the closet. It's some of the best dog food in the city. Kelv asked me to hold it down for 'em. I'll weigh it and see how much it is when I come back later," he mentioned as he grabbed his car keys from the counter, heading out.

The moment she saw his tail lights disappear from the view of the open curtain, she was off into his drugs. She quickly sampled the fine white powder. Indeed, as he mentioned, it was super fire. That shit had her passing gas, anticipating line after line every five minutes.

During the following three days, Peter acted as if he'd totally forgotten he'd given her the drugs.

She felt the hunger of a wolf for it. Her constant nose runs were beyond her ability to hide. As it stands, the finer the dope, the more its drain caused the users nose to run.

For hours, Peter would lay listening to her sniffles while she slept.

By the next Friday morning, he inquired where were the drugs?

She retrieved it from her bra.

"I kept it close by, in case you needed them," she responded.

Peter couldn't believe it. He eased away into the basement and dropped it on his digital scale once again. His eyes narrowed. Kelv was right. "This dope-fiend-ass hoe!" he yelled, staring at the small baggie, hurt at the fact Kelv was right more than anything. Paula had cleverly been refilling the small baggie with pure Domnin to substitute the powder she'd used. Her only mistake was that she never used a scale to weigh it properly. She was eyeballing it and everybody knows eyeballing is never accurate.

Pissed, he stormed through the house looking for her. She always knew when she was about to get the business! A fierce beating from him, to say! She hid in a closet.

"Bitch, where are you? I'mma kill yo' black ass today!" he screamed, gathering her things. First, he snatched her gear from the bedroom dresser drawers and tossed them savagely from the window onto the front lawn into the ongoing pile of flames he lit! He then searched the house for her as he continued to toss her things out every window he passed until his fuse finally popped. He fumbled through the kitchen drawers, tossing every item onto the floor. Instantly, he found what he wanted and carried on through the house.

Thoughtless of the police infested neighborhood and the drugs in his left pocket, he stood on the front lawn tossing more lighter fluid onto the expensive Apple-Bottom, Fendi, Murder-By-Design, C.J. by Cookie Johnson, Gucci heels, furs and more. Bottled in a sea of rage by Paula's betrayal, he eyeballed the flames as they illuminated in a yellow/orange glow.

In Peter's peripheral vision a silhouette of Paula appeared from the upstairs window. Terrified, stripped down to her signature yellow lace bra and panties, she carefully timed Peter's movements coming. She quickly doubled into the few pieces of pricey gear he missed.

And out the bathroom window she went, managing to escape limping away into the shadows of the dumpsters with no clue of how in the hell she was going to feed that growing monkey on her back without Peter's petty cash box, especially after Stinky was now in and out of prison for committing the bullshit crimes over the years, pulling dope-fiend moves for drugs to keep Paula high and close at his side, knowing without a shadow of a doubt that there would come the day she would break and give him that ass he'd been dreaming of since day one.

CHAPTER SEVEN – Fucked With No Grease

Tone anxiously backed into a reserved parking slot and popped the trunk. "Get yo' slick ass out!" he yelled.

The brightness of the morning sun temporarily burned Paula's pupils. Her slender back slumped against the spare tire. She inhaled a refreshing gulp of air. As she exhaled her vision cleared. Her weary, light colored eyes darted right to left fearfully.

"Can't you fuckin' hear straight? Get out!" Tone screamed, gazing over her every move as if she would magically disappear if he'd taken a second to blink.

As she'd once been told, every now and then, everyone wished to be someone else. And at that moment, Lady Paula wished to be anyone other than herself!

What once felt as putty in her hands a couple months prior, to running off with Tone's and his younger brother, Bow's, drugs, weren't no longer all laughs and games as she faced climbing from the trunk of Tone's rental while reminiscing more of her previous days before being caught out on a humbug and enjoying her three week bender scavenging a known heroin track on the Ill-side in the John Deshield Projects.

There was only so much her polluted mind could remember that day. It had only been an hour after she'd so called crept from the rear door of Big Dave's project trap spot when Tone slid behind her, then knocked her unconscious with the butt of the .44 caliber pistol. He carried her quickly to his car, dumped her in, then slammed the trunk over her head. However, her last wish at this moment was to have never met his ass years ago on the porch of Stinky's drug haven.

The thought of Stinky's relieved expression to see her after finding out old boy who was released from prison and said to have had the finest dope, turned out to be her old pal Stinky. She was blown away to see him doing so good after so many years. Although it burned even more, dwelling on the fact he was the one who had introduced her to the very life and was now the cause of her present predicament which caused her to be climbing from Tone's trunk. Stinky welcomed her into his foreign world of 'crazy' on a false promise the powdery drug was harmless. He had lied!

The sound of Tone's voice screaming for her to enter the creepy residence reminded her of the regretful day she had left Stinky's place with him.

The tan brick home resembled a mansion of a famous star. The dwelling was an abandoned three level building. Tone locked her into a dark closet while he prepared her demise. The darkness and terror reminded her of the days she had denied Stinky his desire to have his way with her, as so the other girls. He would then deadbolt them into the house and disconnect the power as his sick way of starving them out until they submitted to his disgusting appetite.

At times it worked.

With or without electricity, the rear yard of Stinky's the hole in the wall was spooky, trashy with cigarette butts trailing the urine smelled gangway. The main floor of the lower apartment was the dwelling of other homeless addicts, such as Paula. They were his best kept treasures, as he thought of them.

His domains were known as the north hood's 'Cubby House.'

How could Paula ever forget Spence and Muff? Two junkies she bonded with during her days of dope sickness. The trio shared drugs, networked deals together and robbed Peter to pay Paul throughout metro St. Louis to East Saint where the tole of 8 to 10 grams of heroin was purchased hourly by Muff, who copped work from a mutual friend of Tone's. Little did Paula know, heroin ruled the black market and Muff, as so many other down low addicts would of crossed out anything in their path chasing another high.

The Mexican mud ran a hundred bucks a gram, unlike the 86% China White the Rush City boys sold at $200 to $300 per gram of synthetic flake. Nevertheless, the tar sold across the Illinois Bridge from Rush City. The White Flake heroin from the Jamaicans was said to have been five times more addictive than the killa STL brown sticky. Who besides Stinky, knew his twisted polluted brain had the ability to cleverly plot out such a perfect set-up on the outskirts of St. Louis', Mark Twain district near the deadly Union Boulevard, housing a string of kick ass gorgeous addicts. The tiny crack and heroin fueled neighborhood held St. Louis' highest national homicide rate, as the *USA Today* read.

Sadly, to stand by and watch a once true friendship wither away before Stinky's eyes, Paula's addiction turned for the worst by the minute, drastically pushing her further into humiliation and immoral acts to the point of her being classified a clear junkie out there sucking young rollers off and begging for her next fix, whereas Stinky somehow became that last man on earth she once swore she'd never sleep with!

Trapped by the claws of Stinky's potent drugs on the one day Paula despised the most; Peter's birthday.

Her empty stomach ached to the core as her eyes closed at the sight of her black lace, *Victoria's Secret*, boy shorts she had worn for the third day.

They were crumbled inside the denim shorts pulled down just above the black rose tatted on her left ankle. Face down in a twerking position, her chipped and broken fingernails tightened at the edge of Stinky's old hand-me-down leather couch, as he entered her tight anus, just as she recalled the same happening years ago one rainy night when she showed her face at Stinky's domain, dope sick.

His disrespectful ass disregarded their friendship in every fashion, scheming, supplying her with all she needed to preserve her diarrhea and stomach cramps only to further drive his nasty penis into her warm, wet flesh.

As the following months ran their course, the pinnacle of Paula's impregnated situation plummeted into the worst. The true hidden serpent, of her first and last friend on earth, slowly displayed Stinky's deadly hand. His conniving ways soon lured her into his merciless beatings, forcing her into prostitution with his special selected hustlers who in turn supplied him. In exchange for a high, he was consciously aware of the power of the hand that rocked the cradle. He continued to execute his humiliating tactics when the girls were short of cash. It was a well balanced toss up of breaking their spirits to keep them in bondage to, and under, his spell. Most of the girls, except Paula, unknowingly shot the heroin in every portion of their bodies using the same HIV infected syringes purely out of drug dumb ignorance. In his eyes, Paula was only yet to start jerking the needle! When that day came he planned to rip her half-hip ass a new ass the minute she did.

Although he shared her addiction, the white heroin habit was much worse on women than men. Stinky knew of this long before he'd introduced Paula to the killer powdery drug.

"How in the hell do I always find myself trapped in these crazy dilemmas with my hands tied, fucking with these crazy, no good, trapped in the closet niggas?" she questioned her inner conscience, figuratively speaking. Since it had been only months since she'd last recalled paying a visit to the women's prison where she swore to her dear mother, then and there, all those cardinal lies she'd hear of her from those gossiping prison whores weren't true and that she was on point living with a friend. Pam knew better. Hell was Paula's last name.

Now, totally alone, trapped in this dark closet, within Paula's innocent soul she wished to still be housed in that rehabilitation center instead of begging for her life in Tone's dark closet of Hell, knowing she was about to die. She'd rather been anywhere on earth, even if it meant being back home dealing with those old pesky male rehab nurses, fondling her night and day, which only led her to relapse and never to return.

In speaking of those conditions, the only true whereabouts she would rather have been, happened to be that memorable McDonald's she used as a sanctuary before and after her sexual encounters and avoiding Stinky and his mad spells, bursting his way through the Cubby shack's unhinged door, demanding sex from those caught with their panties off, showering, during the occasions he was filled with alcohol and out of the tasty dog-food to exchange for their services.

How could she forget the incidents when he watched her from his window after she denied him sex? He knew her well. It was just her defying him, wanting special treatment, drifting into her altered ego thing, acting as if she had a set of nuts, storming out the back door. Paula recalled doing so one moonless night on her baby sister's belated birthday.

As a surprise to herself, she recalled the day she went cold turkey on the never ending drug for over a record breaking sixteen hours; being sick of Stinky's BS, she trotted across the alleyway headed towards the faint glow from the small McDonald's parking lot. Just as she made it to the doors of the establishment, rumbling sounds bolted over her shoulders from a candy painted heroin-tan Porsche truck skidding into the parking slot behind her as she entered the glass doors. You could say she cared less who the thirsty driver was hunking for her attention. She rushed to the rest room, locking herself inside and suddenly, as she sat into the first stall, burying her confused head into her lap, wishing her baby sister a happy B-Day.

A few minutes later progressively rapid knocks rattled the door.

"Almost done!" she yelled. She raked her wet fingers through her tangled dirty hair. "Done!" She smiled as she pulled the door open; her eyes bulged instantly. She swayed on her feet in shame; Peter was there staring at her.

His eyes popped! "Look at what we have here!" he said giggling, grabbing at his crotch, groping himself until his penis started to rise.

Paula attempted to brush past him. He blocked her path!

'Where was Stinky's slick ass when she needed him?' she thought.

"Let me look at you!" Peter growled, lifting her chin, pouring his eyes over her like anthrax.

"I see yo' ass dun turned into a full bloom junkie, huh?" he grunted.

For the first time, Peter was right. Paula was washed up! The lovely chocolate stunna accompanied him raised a shameful brow towards Paula's appearance.

"Don't tell me this the one you was so crazy about?" the woman asked.

He laughed.

Paula quickly glanced at her replacement. As Paula once was, the young stunna was breathtaking, rocking a fitted red mini skirt and killer BB stilettos.

She was a southern belle thick as her home girl, K. Michelle, with deep dimples and a name such as Val-Val.

"Val, wait for me out in the whip, I need to holla at her about some

Paypa!" he lied.

Val-Val, being so crazy in love, she giggled as she stepped past Paula.

She scented of expensive vanilla Dolce and Gabana fragrance as Paula once had. Tears fell from her eyes as she slid her lips over the head of the stiff meat in a spit sloppy twist motion, the way she knew he loved it.

Paula wanted his ugly ass to disappear without that bag in this hand. She knew she had to get busy fast to get rid of his crooked, roach-leg dick ass! She watered her throat and slid her God given lips over him faster.

He stood there enjoying the feel of face fucking her as if he were deep off into some good good from South Beach.

She gagged as he grinded deeper down her throat. Silently, she cried the entire ordeal. He nearly fell to his knees lost in another sarcastic laugh as his cream filled and flooded her mouth. He couldn't help it. Her jaw felt better than ever before at the thought of her still being so accessible for his disposal. Just as he skeeted in her face his cold hearted ass smacked her face with the tiny baggie as he hurried to join his chocolate stunna.

Dehumanized, Paula closed herself in the stall, locking it from the inside trembling in tears. Her soul totally weakened, she heard the faint music over the bus line vibrating the McDonald's walls. She had sat there lost, sniffling back tears until she was sure the Porsche was gone. At that point, all she wanted was one of three things; to taste that powder in her hand, to be in jail with her mother, or in the ground lying beside her twin sister.

Now, it seemed Tone was surely about to send her to the grave, except she wouldn't be lying beside her sister.

Life in Paula's confused perspective rested on a suicidal decline. She was using so much heroin she thought the day would come when it would all end. Mostly considering that she would OD and leave her regrets and problems behind for Stinky and Peter to live with; considering all they'd done to her to put her where she was. In a manner of speaking, as if it had all happened yesterday, she recalled the day she had met Tone, the warm evening she rested on the porch of Stinky's Cubby house and the metallic red Mustang parked at the curb. The 5/11 man exited the sports car, rocking a True Religion button down and baggy pants. He was a handsome, dark skinned, thuggish stud with corn rows and Cartier shades. He stepped to Paula with a cell phone glued to his face. "Sue Woo!" he said, ending his call.

"Hello," Paula said, batting her naturally long lashes.

"What's up Sweetie, let's hit a few corners and kill that edge you got!"

She smiled and stood to her feet happily.

"Ma name Tony, what they call you other than sexy?"

"Paula," she replied with a smile, following him to his vehicle. He was a gentleman. He opened her door, she climbed in.

"Damn, this boy-head bitch bad! Um finna gut that shit, sizz business!" he thought. Tone had taken her home and cleaned her up.

He gave her his ex-bitch Taran's clothes. By the time his little brother came through, she scented in *Imperial*, by Britney Spears, covered with Taran's new Mary Kay silk panties and Tone's 5x, thick T-shirt. The minute Bow arrived he chewed at his lips dropping the duffle bag at his feet. Her feet were small and yummy with cherry polish. Her hair was wet and wavy as always.

The scent of Tone's dope dick lingered with her juices. His 22 year old brother was no match for Paula. Her wild eyes were glued to that bag he dropped at his feet.

She beckoned him over. 'I gotta make sure he never thinks of that bag again!' she thought fast. Then to totally distract him, she slowly slid her index finger deeply into her pink trimmed slit with ease. As was the old lil' Kim, Paula was overwhelmingly sexual, too. Not only that, but Paula swallowed, as most men preferred. Her slit produced juices onto her fingers. She licked them lustfully! Bow's eyes locked on those shiny wet fingers. His breath lodged in his throat as she erotically sucked more of her own sweet nectar from them. The front of his True Religion jean shorts tightened as his passion rose.

"Oh, is all that for me, Daddy?" she teased, pointing at the bulge in his shorts.

Bow had no chance. Paula invited him into her sex room. His eyes fluttered as she blessed him with the finest cap the kid had ever endured. She held his small balls in her right palm up to her chin and mumbled to him that he was the largest and best she'd ever had as she sucked him savagely.

"Oh shit!" he jumped.

Her lengthy tongue teased his balls like a snake trainer. This time, he didn't jump. Paula turned the kid out in that living room after it was all said and done.

"Baby, go and run us some bath water. I wanna hit that dick in the tub!" she said.

He moved fast. Bow's passion caused him to run like he was landing his 747 penis on Paula's slick and well lubricated landing strip. But to Paula, his penis was nothing but a small private plane crashing into an ocean of hungry sharks. She watched his buff body disappear through the door as if into a mist. She seized the duffle bag, took a peek into it to make sure her lick was on point. At the sight of the drugs the corner of her mouth foamed. She listened for the shower to begin.

"I'm out this bitch!" she mumbled as she made her exit in fast creeping barefooted steps for dope heaven and dear life. The heavy door was left ajar. Bow returned naked to see what took ole girl so long.

"No, no, no!" he shouted as his eyes darted to the spot he had laid the Gucci bag containing the quarter kilo of uncut heroin.

Paula hit hard; real hard. That fatal mistake stormed her mind after Tone drug her out her spot and then kicked - knocked her unconscious again. He had to make a run to the city to pick up his brother, Bow.

CHAPTER EIGHT – Dead Alive

Present day, four hours later...

The boys returned. Paula was once again awakened from her trance finding herself now lying face down on the cold floor.

Tone and Bow both sat in folding chairs, staring at her. She looked around, not recognizing her surroundings. The side of her face was red and swollen. The pain was screaming, '*Do something! Do something!*' Paula decided not to scream. There would be no one within ear shot to save her anyway.

Tone slowly sat her up and she wrapped her arms around her knees.

"Bitch, why you trying to hide that trashy ass pussy? You ain't hide that shit when you ran off with ma shit! Did'ja?" Bow screamed.

He stepped to her and stomped her face so hard she tumbled onto her bruised side in a spasm.

"Shut up hoe, before I do it again!" he shouted furiously, laughing in spite of her terror and salty tears, which were running like a rainy November day in Memphis. "You gonna wish you were dead before we done with cho slick ass, bitch!"

The evil smile crackled through his voice frightening her even more than the words he spoke. She lowered her head against the floor and cried. Bow was a gorilla unchained with a thirst for her blood only.

To prevent his aggressive outrage, Paula lifted her hips, allowing his kick to slide under her. Her chance of escape was already decided.

Tone walked up and stood over her staring gladly into her pitiful face contemplating what he really wanted to do with her being that their location was off grip in the heart of Joplin, Missouri. Plus, the moon was full on this night.

"I'ma fuck'er ass!" Bow said, deciding to slam his filthy penis inside of her anus for the first and last time she'd ever feel raw meat. Tone hit the lights as he exited the room, leaving Bow to handle this whore however he felt she deserved. He knew it wouldn't be good for her.

Tone returned to his line of drinks and E-pills. Bow, on the other hand, drug the girl into the darkness of the back porch. The total cost of his drugs was coming out of her ass, literally. He sodomized her.

As the huge gangsta did so, Paula closed her eyes, remembering the last time she had been forced to have anal sex as Bow forced his way into her anus.

Her brain twirled back to the morning of May 18th, approximately 6:37am, where she sat homeless, hidden in the bushes of the McDonald's rear parking lot. It was the only place she knew of with such a large garbage can which enabled her to sneak into it after hours for leftover food to eat and hustle for drugs. Usually, at exactly 4:30pm, the night manager, Carlos, would dump the leftover meals into the can for the young girl to feast upon. But this time, the sex craved employer watched her as he'd done for months.

Like clockwork Paula attacked the dumpster as if she was a

California Condor, snatching and grabbing all her small hands could carry. As she climbed into the dumpster this time, she felt something lurking cold and fast over her shoulder as Carlos made his move. As usual, he had laid and played on her hunger as you would any other rodent. He had studied the monitors in his office to the hidden cameras outside. At the sight of her, then moving quickly, within seconds, he stood behind her.

"Hey!" he yelled, scaring her.

Paula cowered about to make a run for it.

"What are you doing?" he yelled.

"Nothing!" she swore in shock with a bag of still warm food clenched in her fist.

"Looks like stealing to me! I'mma have to call the police, I guess!" he stated devilishly.

She looked away at the empty lot and recalled seeing him leave minutes before she made her move. He'd waited around the corner this time, she guessed.

The parking lot called out to her. '*Run!*' it demanded.

Again, from the small lot to the bushes and from the bushes to the gangways around them called to her to run! She was too shook up to haul ass as she wanted to and knew she should!

Carlos jerked the bag from her hand as she stepped toward him. He quickly led her into the restaurant, making it perfectly clear he wanted head and sex with her or else she was on her way to jail for stealing.

As they entered, he eagle gripped her ass and enjoyed how it shook and clapped noticeably as if she had something stuck in it.

There was no doubt, even then, she was at the lowest point of her life. Her spine tightened, knowing what was coming, as he covered his penis in KY Jelly and went to sliding in and out of her rectum. Every inch of her wanted to laugh at his small size. She thought he would bust her open, but he didn't.

At that moment, tears covered her eyes as Bow disgraced her over a bale of hay while she reminisced about that fucked up situation while Bow ripped even harder into her anus disregarding her tears and the spots of blood that stuck to her butt cheeks. The more Bow tried to devour her anus, the more she searched her thoughts to that awful day at McDonald's as Bow constantly hammered into her vindictively.

Carlos, the manager of that McDonald's, had punished her over his work desk. Afterwards, she had asked, as she pulled her lace panties back up to her waist, if he could spare a few dollars. The low life manager treated her as if she were a lost whore. He gave her ten dollars for the most wonderful nut he ever splashed over anyone's lower back.

'Ten fuckin' dollars? For real?' she said to herself. *'The bastard basically raped me and just walked away laughing!'* She bottled the urge to curse him out. She had limped through the parking lot as the pain became unbearable. Carlos had given her an 800mg Ibuprofen. She took it and rushed to purchase a ten dollar pill from a hood star named Foot-Loc. She knew of him from a gang called 5/7 Case Mob. Only then did the pain subside until her high went down. What happened to her was a regular hustle for dope craving young girls.

"Bitch get up!" Bow screamed, breaking her daydream as he pulled himself out and released his claws from her backside, tapping the head of his penis at the crack of her round slit. His explosion dripped from the lining of her clitoris.

Tone decided he was through monkeying around with her. He stormed onto the back porch and was relieved to witness his B-dog giving Paula's scandalous ass just what she deserved. She yelped in deep pain. Bow stood over her, urinating into her face. Paula tried blocking it with her forearms and hands.

''What the fuck you doing, Blood?" Tone asked.

"B, fuck this trash! I'ma piss down her throat!" Bow looked crazy. In fact, there was no doubt he was off. He planted his foot into her face with force.

White spots exploded in her eyes. She fell unconscious again. A small pool of blood formed under her mouth, as some leaked out.

"Blood, hand me that blade. I'm going to gut this hoe like a fish. Then we can dump her ass by the creek, B."

Tone nodded his head in approval and went to get the blade. No sooner had he returned, Bow hatefully stabbed her in the chest. Blood gushed out of her nude body. Coming around she screamed for mercy but none was shown.

"Please, no! Please don't kill me!" she shouted as the 12 inch blade plunged into her again and again. The boys continued working her over. Bow pushed the point into her until it scraped the concrete beneath her. Bow had another turn. He slashed her and Paula's body trembled and gagged for air.

After the fact, the brothers tossed her naked body from their Grannie's old Ford pickup and into a corn field. At that very moment Paula's spirit was face to face with an image of her own bleeding body. Her eyes were wide open, staring back at herself. The girl had been stabbed at a count of fifteen times over her entire body. She wasn't sure if she was breathing or floating in mid air. Her body was unresponsive.

"Oh my God. Am I dead?"

"Not yet, you're not," Carla's spirit answered.

Paula twisted her head fast to the sound of a familiar voice. No one was there. She then heard distant giggling.

"I'm dead and going crazy!" Paula thought with both hands folded over her forehead.

"Yeah, you're crazy all right. Running around here, using drugs, eating out of the trash can and whoring for those low lives!"

"Who the hell is that girl? God, are you a girl?" Paula asked, looking around.

This made the feminine voice stroke Paula's face. She started to run. A bright light surrounded her. It was a familiar and warm feeling. She smiled. She knew then who it was.

"Carla!" she screamed.

"Hey, Ms. Lady," the spirit spoke. Paula could feel her tears burning her eyes. They seemed asleep.

"Carla, I'm so glad they killed me. Now we can be together, lil sis," Paula said.

"Paula, I'm not going to let you die,"

"What?" she yelled.

"What about momma? She's suffering in that place praying for you."

Paula reached out to the mist.

"Ms. Lady, you need to get it together now! I'm so disappointed in you. Carrying on through life trying to accomplish something you face. Lying on your back for every single dude that comes your way. What happened to that tough as nails big sister that once protected me?"

Paula was at a loss for words.

"I'm watching you. Don't let me down again, big Sister."

The light around Paula began to dim.

"Carla!" she yelled.

"I love you Ms. Lady. Remember, I'm watching you."

The voice sounded so distant now. Paula could feel the warmth fade away with Carla's voice.

A dog barking sounded faintly from the distance. A small boy chased the pooch playfully. The dog sniffed Paula's face and began licking it eagerly. The young boy came running to the grey bloodhound's findings.

"What'cha got, Chunky?" he asked before reaching Paula's body. "Oh, God!" he screamed, turning his head towards Paula's naked body. His lungs pumped louder for his father's help.

At the yell from his Son, Mr. McDaniels came running through the woods with his shotgun up and ready to fire. Seeing Paula's nude and bloody body the older man reached forward, checking for a pulse on her arm.

"Lordy, she's alive. Run, go call 911!" he added, toward his son.

CHAPTER NINE – Returned Angel

"Wake up!" a voice whispered, seemingly directly into her ear.

Paula was in the intensive care unit of Barnes Jewish Hospital. Her eyelids seemed to be glued shut. The clock on the wall read 9:20 A.M. The pleasant, hauntingly familiar, voice soothed Paula's runaway heart. Luckily for her, she had been delivered to and treated at this hospital, in which she had received first class care. Her doctors were the best and brightest in the facility. Even though her wounds were life threatening and after losing so much blood, the paramedics had even whispered, 'she's a goner' when they delivered her to the emergency room but she survived.

Now, for several months Paula had remained in a coma. The machines were connected to her monitoring her breathing, heart rate and blood pressure. Her I.V. made sure she was fed nutritiously. The doctors were in and out every few hours monitoring and tracking her progress, nutrition and brain activity.

She had received no visitors. No one called inquiring about her. Her nurses found that strange. 'How could a woman so beautiful not be missed?' they asked each other.

The heroin was long gone out of Paula's system and her natural beauty had returned. The bags under her eyes had faded away and her weight had increased drastically. Her lips had found their way back to their natural pink and her skin magically cleared and became as smooth as a cover girl's model; easy and breezy.

Paula was like Brandy, brand new. All except the ½ inch scar at the base of her left temple. She would wear it forever, unless it was fixed cosmetically. She had lain on that hospital bed and metamorphosed into the beautiful young woman she had been born to be.

"Wake up!" the voice echoed.

Something was using the sunlight to travel through her. She felt its eyes on her.

"Wake up Ms. Lady!" Carla's voice boomed in her head like a loud speaker.

Her body jerked and the heart monitor suddenly came to life and began running like a marathon. It was a beautiful day. Not a dark cloud in the sky. The trees were fresh and spring green.

"Get up Paula!" she heard herself say this time. Her eyes began fluttering.

She could hear Carla's giggling as she felt strange warm waves massaging her face.

Suddenly, Paula was stumbling through the dark forest of her mind. She wore only a white nightgown. However, there was just darkness! The leaves and branches were black instead of green. She willed herself to hear her sister's giggles. She stepped between dark stones. She could feel the wind blowing against her. She felt a dark presence. It was coming, but something drove her forward. She felt the pull of the darkness behind her as she ran towards the pull of the clouds that had formed in front of her.

"Run now!" Carla's voice screamed.

Paula felt her bare feet moving swiftly. She stumbled through the glowing cloud.

"Wake up!" again, Carla yelled in Paula's ear.

Her eyes snapped open ... she blinked as they burned for a long moment. She moved them, looking slowly to the right, then the left. She used her peripheral vision to better see the unfamiliar faces that stood afar. Colors exploded in her eyes as everything went from black and white to full color. She suddenly felt an overwhelming lightning bolt of rage pierce her thoughts of the faulty reality of the life she'd been living. She was furious, disappointed and wanted to just scream, shout and howl from the agonizing pain that surrounded and threatened to overcome her sanity. She felt the sting of tears burning the inside of her eyelids.

The nurses spoke in hushed tones around her as they fussed over her.

"A survivor of such a brutal assault." she heard them say with pleasure and she felt extremely lucky that the small boy and his sweet, nosy puppy had stumbled upon her.

"Blessed," the doctors had been saying about her, due to the fact that the knife wounds should have ended her life, yet, she survived.

The damage to her liver and kidneys from the knife wounds were almost the cause of her death.

Doctor Ernistine Mitchell was the brightest and youngest in her department.

She looked stuntastically hot in her white smock and flowery hospital scrubs and white Gucci sneakers. She had the darkest colored eyes and black bouncy hair that Paula had ever seen. Doctor Mitchell was that business when it came down to being an independent diva. The nurses called her Doctor Stripper in secret.

Paula wondered how someone so young could have graduated med school so fast. Dr. Mitchell's, aka Diamond, hands were soft as she rubbed Paula's cheek.

"Good to have you back, Doll! I worried about you for a minute."

It took Paula almost two years of therapy to recover. Her body, being young, healed wonderfully.

Diamond was compassionate and against hospital regulations, she snuck her patients food from home. During these two years Paula and Diamond became good friends. Late at night, Diamond would spend hours in Paula's room listening to her life tales of her drug addiction. There were many minutes of tears shared. However, there were more times they would laugh until their ribs hurt and their cheeks reddened. When Diamond had her serious face on, she resembled Lisa Ray. Her smile always lit the room.

"Why don't you have a man?" Paula asked. "I know these niggaz are lined up around the corner after you girl!"

Dropping her voice to a mere hush, Diamond replied, "Really, I don't want a man at the moment. I have enough issues holding down my husband, Courtney, in the feds."

"Girl, you take care of a nigga in jail?" Paula asked.

"Yes!" Diamond admitted. "Sister, that's what we're suppose to do as strong black women! See, let me share one thing with you. That's one of the sole reasons we're losing so many good brothers to them she devils.

"Sid! A white bitch ain't got nothing on this pussy!" Paula added.

They laughed.

"No, seriously, holding down yo' man has much greater value than a good fuck, girl. He could get a good piece of ass anywhere, Honey!" Diamond spoke the truth. "You see, even the weakest white bitch gone travel them miles to see her nigga when he's bitten." And that's one thing I make sure I pride myself in for mine! So if you plan to keep him, you better learn how to treat him!" Diamond ended on that note.

Paula nodded to agree.

It was real talk coming from a vet. Diamond was only 28. She hadn't had sex in months. Her focus had been on bringing Paula back from the dead.

"I gotta get you some dick, girl!" Paula noted.

Diamond smiled.

The next three weeks passed. Diamond had begun preparing

Paula's release party. The staff fussed over Paula as they shared the cake and French Vanilla ice cream. The small get together was a first for the hospital. Never had the Black-Out staff ever given a patient a farewell party so huge. Everyone had grown so attached to Paula and had all rooted for her recovery.

At the end of their lavish party, Diamond presented Paula with a box wrapped in pink paper covered with a huge bow. "Don't open it until everyone leaves," she whispered and winked.

Paula couldn't wait until they left. She tore into the box like a child on Christmas morning.

Diamond watched her.

She hadn't said much at all since the nurses left. Paula looked at the single brass key lying face up in the box. She returned her gaze to Diamond.

"That's the front door key to my place. Your new home if you want it to be," said Diamond.

Paula rushed her and wrapped her arms around her as tears filled their eyes. Paula exhaled, finally. She had been unable to sleep, worrying concerning her living situation and putting some hot one's into those goons that tried to earth her.

She closed her eyes that night and had sweet dreams, knowing when she opened them, it would be a day closer to the rebirth of her twin sister. She promised that Carla would live through her.

CHAPTER TEN – Sister Hood

Paula reached Diamond's house a few hours after her release from the hospital. Diamond had also given Paula the keys to her BMW followed by a hug. The sun shone bright. Paula looked like a million dollars. She wore a loose summer dress, Valentino and Sergion Rossi peep toe pumps. She scented of mangoes and Elizabeth Taylor fragrance. Staring at herself in the rear view mirror of the Beamer with a devious smile she was impressed with the new glowing image she saw. Her face had cleared into flawless radiance. Besides the scar on her left temple, she looked fantastic. She closed her eyes and mentally envisioned her sister Carla's face; the last of it she could remember. Paula had decided, Carla would always be her guiding light and voice of reason.

"Sky's the limit!" Paula said.

She drove around the city envisioning everything through new eyes, as if she were reborn. Every time she stopped at a red light, hot dudes shot their best shot at the diva. She basked in the attention.

She pulled into the drive-thru of Steak-N-Shake and ordered a large strawberry shake and fries. She had been craving that shake so badly. She'd even had a dream of it once. Paula almost felt she was going to cum when she placed the cold spoon onto her warm tongue.

"Mmm!" she moaned.

She punched Diamond's address in the GPS gadget she had installed on the Beamer's dashboard. She followed the voice that boomed out the speakers, leading her through the city. Paula's mouth fell into her lap when she turned into Diamond's neighborhood. The complex was filled with expensive condos and exotic whips. The city's landscape had taken on a new development. The recession had served its purpose both good and bad and Diamond was living well through the hard work and even harder schooling. It was paying off as she was one of Missouri's youngest and most talented african american surgeons.

The streets were freshly paved and the sidewalk was of newly placed tan/red bricks. The landscaping resembled something viewed on MTV Cribs. The trees were dogwood. Their white flowers with blood red tipped petals blossomed on them spectacularly. Some said the red represented the blood of Christ.

Paula knew she didn't know, but only thought of them being beautiful.

The exterior of the condominiums with attached double garages were painted in various light pastel spring colors.

Diamond's french doors were powder blue with outings and marble sills. The outer walls were French Vanilla white. Paula disarmed the security system as she read the code from the pink stationary paper she held between her thin fingers. She toured the house like a spellbound child. Her image reflected from all the shiny appliances throughout the huge kitchen.

Over her head there were solar panels Diamond had installed. The microwave's clock read 2:01. She continued on her exploration through the layout in a wonderful amazement. Diamond had an elevator in the living room that took Paula to the second level of luxury.

"Oh my God!" Paula flabbergastically screamed when her eyes toured the room as she stepped from the elevator onto a Prussian carpet. She had never, in real life, seen a home so beautiful! The little girl came pouring out of her. She pulled her pumps off and mussed her feet into the texture of the soft fabric. She massaged the carpet with her toes. She peeped into the master bedroom. It was to die for!

She called Diamond from the prepaid cell phone that lay on the bed, beside $700 in cash.

"Oh my fucking God!"

Diamond giggled in amusement.

"Bitch, you living like Oprah up in this bitch!"

"Did you take the elevator to the lower level and see your room yet?" Diamond asked.

"Not yet. I'll call you right back," Paula returned.

She ran to the elevator and descended to the lower level, excited. The bell rang and the door opened. Paula screamed in delight. She blinked a few times and pinched her upper arm to make sure she wasn't dreaming. She was looking at a beautiful marble fountain. The lights caused the water to appear tropic. She could feel the cool moisture of the water mist tingling on her face.

She walked slowly around the marble fountain. In the left corner lay a full length wine bar equipped with wooden bar stools and a large mirror behind it. The floors were also marble. Paula checked the first door she came to.

It was a huge closet. The second room she found was a lovely lounging room with an expensive Sony washer and dryer. It had a leather sofa and flat screen 72" HD-6 Plasma. The third door she pushed open was the jackpot.

She walked into the plush room and hit the light switch. In the middle of the floor was an all black steel canopy bed with dark Prada curtains hanging all around. Mounted into the wall was a 64" Zenith life size projection television. In the corner was a complete Apple computer and color printer filled with photos of Paula before and after surgery. The room was lined in the fluffiest black carpet. Paula opened the walkin closet. She fell to her knees crying in long sniffles. She called Diamond back, which only brought more tears to her face.

"I love you! Thank you D!" Paula said, buffing her tears away.

Diamond retrieved the single tear that danced down her cheek. "I love you more Angel. And stop being such a wussy!" she replied.

Paula smiled, staring into the closet as her tears continued. The walk in closet was filled with the latest fashions bearing price ranges from $487 jeans to $3,600 Zyion dresses dazzling as if she were at a clearance sale at Lasuook. Paula loved rocking fly gear and it had been ever so long since her body enjoyed any. Peter's face immediately flashed through her mind.

Later that night, Diamond returned home. Paula awaited with the damnedest surprise of her own for Diamond, which sat next to her. He was muscularly built in his skin tight T-shirt and skinny jeans. Some would say an alpha-male at the least! His hair was naturally brunette with a bald fade. He had jade gray eyes. Diamond looked at Paula who now stood and led her into the kitchen.

"What in the world do you got that man in our home for, Paula?" Diamond noted, staring over at him warily from where she stood. "Even though, he got his lil' Boris Kojor thing going on, being he mixed an all," she mumbled.

"Girl, you move too fast for me!"

They'd already discussed a 'no men allowed' rule.

"Stop it Diamond. You know he's hot!"

Diamond agreed slowly.

"Good. Cause he's for you, as a matter of fact!" said Paula.

Diamond's eyes widened. She shook her head no! Paula pushed the issue. She wasn't taking no for an answer, especially now that she had just spent $950 on his ass! She received the money from the other nurses on the day of her release that each one placed bills in their cards. They were such sweethearts! She would never forget them.

"I'm not playing. Now go freshen up! He's going to rock yo' world, girl," Paula added.

"Bitch, did you do anything with him?" Diamond had to know.

"No!"

"I mean, I was just checkin', cause Ms. Ego don't do sloppy seconds!" she lied.

Before Diamond could utter another word, Paula turned her back. She left the room with a nasty walk that she couldn't help. Her ass seemed to shake and clap all within a single motion. Diamond smiled as she ran into her elevator.

Fifteen minutes later she emerged from her elegant bathroom dressed in a Korean silk robe. She saw the naked stud laying in the middle of her bed.

The CD player played Kelly Rollin Remix *Motivation*, featuring Usher and Busta Rhymes. He stripped her and lifted her off her feet. Her breath got caught in her throat. It had been ages since she had given that pussy up.

It was as ripe as a virgin on prom night! She was soaking wet by the time he got her fully open.

Outside the room, Paula tiptoed and stood beyond the door listening to her pleas of stop, no more, it hurt, put'ma legs down until she trembled into an orgasm spill. Paula silently pumped a fist on the D.L. like Serena Williams does when she wins the Wimbledon.

Within an hour after the masculine stud got it in and performed his paid duty, in Diamond's no longer sacred lair, he exited, followed by her on wobbly legs. She quickly found the sofa and planted her locked-up husband behind her. Matt had given her a memorable spanking!

Paula covered her mouth to his and her laughter.

Diamond smiled. She knew Paula had to have known ole' boy punished that ass!

Paula escorted the male stripper out of the condo. As they were strolling to his car, he dug into his pocket for his truck keys. An empty pill bottle hit the gravel.

Paula stopped in her track. "What's those?" she asked. "You sick or something

He laughed. "No, those were my last Viagra's, baby girl. That shit is hard to come by nowadays," he stated with a smile.

"What do you mean?" she asked.

"I mean Viagra and Oxicotton and other prescription pills is the new crazy now. You ain't heard?" "N'all that's not the vogue drug in Hustle City?"

"Sorry!" Paula shrugged her shoulders.

"Well, out here where people have real money, it is he who has pills gets rich and that's a fact!" he added.

"OK, let's just say, if I could get some, will you help me sell them?"

"Hell yeah! Ain't no question! Of course, I want a cut."

Paula nodded in agreement as Superman drove away in his Audi. Her mind was downloading as fast as a net-ten access code as she returned inside.

"So, how ya feel?" she started to say when she came back into the house. Diamond's light snoring answered her question. She was curled up like a sleeping snake holding her floor pillow. Paula retrieved a blanket and covered her with it. She then stepped to her computer. She punched at the small keys fast! She logged online and Googled illegal prescription drugs for the next two hours while Diamond slept. She went to *Pillschool@.org* online.

She had learned that Oxycodone, pronounced by most as *Oxycotton,* was one of the most powerful pain medications ever! Viagra was also a prescribed sex enhancing pill that's been sweeping the nation blind.

"This white people shit!" she thought. Something caught her eye immediately.

A pop up display about cocaine. She hit enter, and a new screen covered her Window 7. It showed an arrest of some white man named Scott Myers who lived near Diamond. It read that Scott Mayor had been busted in an undercover sting operation and charged with possession of cocaine with the intent to distribute and racketeering involving large quantities of cocaine. There was a picture of him with a girl. Paula's eyes narrowed.

She clicked on the photo to enlarge. She knew the smiling girl in that picture with him.

It was Linda, her P.M. nurse. She happened to be one of Paula's fave five.

The very next day, Paula came strolling into the hospital dressed to kill.

She had to show the girls what a good job they'd done saving her life. She wore a silk Donna Karan dress with a matching Jimmy Choo diamond clutch bag. Her stilettos were diamond patterned with a glittering sequined Jimmy Choo fur strap around her ankles. Her hair was swept up into a bun on top of her head with a few dangling curls in front of her ears which made her look exotic. She had blossomed into a true treasure. Where she had once been insecure, she now had swag and oodles of it!

"Oh my God!" Tonya, the I.C.N. secretary, screamed as she stood from her desk holding files, absolutely blown away by the smile on Paula's face.

"Hey girl!" Paula shouted.

"Baby, don't just stand there! Come, come!" Tonya motioned her hands, inviting Paula into the *Staff's Only* area. Their discussion faded away as they walked through the white doors.

"Surprise!"

"Ahh!" Linda's scream startled the other staff.

Everyone turned and rushed Paula with open arms!

"Girl, how have you been?" they wanted to know.

Paula's, Queen Perfume filled the room. "I'm fine. Y'all knew I had to come see my favorite bitches!"

Certainly it was time for a special R.N. break. The group of women walked quickly through the hospital, heading for the designated smoking area outside. They were gossiping and chattering like childhood friends. They made such a fuss over who's Paula's number one godmother!

"Gloria, I absolutely love that green eyeliner on you! It makes you look so much younger!" Paula commented, examining Gloria's long, naturally dark eyelids. She held her face gently.

"Thank you, baby. You're the only one that noticed." She rolled her eyes over the faces of the others.

"Bitch, I noticed two days ago, I just didn't wanna make you think it was some kind of competition with me!" Linda added, tossing her long, dark, rich, bouncy hair, teasing Gloria.

They laughed in fun.

"I couldn't ask for more. I could honestly say this time, I'm blessed and you are a part of the sole reason I smile today!" Paula truly felt.

"Girl, stop it!" Gloria objected immediately. "You gone make me mess up my eyeliner!"

"I know, but ya'll just don't understand. When I was almost dead, you girls gave me hope. I heard every word of hope and encouragement and sometimes when y'all would leave me, I would cry and wonder why I couldn't have a mother like you Gloria, or sisters like Linda, or you, Evelyn, and forever Diamond and Tona." Paula sniffed back her remaining tears. "I love y'all with all my heart!" she swore.

"Oh damn!" Gloria said as her tears streaked her eyeliner down her cheeks.

The other girls showed their emotions as well. Paula's gaze was intent.

"If any of you ever need me, I'm there, no questions asked!" Paula added, "I mean, if y'all need ya husband whacked, I can make it happen!"

This changed their moods.

"I think I'll stand in that line," Evelyn joked playfully.

The ladies burst out in a loud crying laughter. Paula caught Linda's attention quickly.

"At last," said Paula, smiling faintly. "Let me have a word with you alone, Linda."

She nodded. The ladies stepped a couple feet away out of anyone's earshot.

"Nice to be able to talk to someone and not worry about Ms. Know-It-All ear fucking you!" she spoke of Tonya. "I need to, like, talk to you away from here!"

Linda promised to pick Paula up from Diamond's spot at 5 P.M., once she got off work. Paula exchanged cell phone numbers with the girls and Gloria snapped pictures of Paula with her digital camera. She stored them in her home electronic picture frames that lined her hallway walls. Paula let the girls get back to their work. She high-tailed it home where she would finish connecting the dots between the man busted for all those drugs and Linda...

CHAPTER ELEVEN – The Come Up

When Paula opened her eyes, she wasn't sure where she was. Suddenly, she realized she was still in the passenger seat of Linda's silver Lamborghini. Linda had the A/C blasting on chill. It had put Paula to sleep. The exact same questions she remembered thinking before she'd fallen asleep was the same one that stagnated her thoughts after she awoke. 'How in the hell does an R.N. afford a new Gallarado with custom work done?' Not to mention the interior was Flipmode Outrageous with a Nia Long brown candy paint job.

Paula knew immediately what it was as they pulled into Linda's driveway.

"This bitch getting it!" Paula swore under her breath. She curiously eyeballed the petite dominican and black diva. The house was 5,500 square feet of pure magic. The outer walls were made of clear glass. From the driveway,

Paula could see the living room. Once inside, she sat on a large, black Zyion leather sofa. Linda had all black everything. She was highly race conscious.

"Oh shit!" Paula yelped, then folded her legs and put her feet on the couch when Tiger ran into the room.

The small puppy sat a couple feet away staring at Paula, then Linda. The red-nose pit bull's attitude was of non-hostility just one of bewildered confusions.

'Who is she?' Tiger seemed to ask cocking his head first one way, then the other.

Linda bounced on one foot removing one shoe, then the other. She threw her white Princess Reeboks and Tiger took off as usual, retrieving both sneakers playfully. Once the puppy disappeared with the sneakers hung from his mouth, Paula looked at Linda.

"Oh, he's a sweetheart! He's finna take mommy's shoes to the closet." She stood at the fireplace with one shoulder propped against the mantel. Tiger came running. His round gray eyes fluffed at Paula.

"Come here boy!"

Linda picked the happy puppy up and sat beside Paula. Her fingers frisked through Tiger's muscular hair. The puppy dove off Linda's lap into Paula's.

"Traitor!" Linda laughed. "So, what's bothering you, Doll? What is it, money?" Linda asked.

"Yeah, like a million bucks and this house. Oh, and that Lambo outside," Paula replied, then giggled. She went on to tell her girl about seeing her face on the net affiliated with Scotty. The conversation gave her leeway to bring up the cocaine issue. Linda couldn't deny her evidence.

"Yeah, that was indeed my big shot boyfriend. Had he not been such a show off he would still be with us, but oh no! Scotty had to be seen by the world. Girl you know how men hate to listen to women!"

Paula listened as Linda vented. "So sis, tell me, how could I score some coke, where as I could make a little money?"

Linda frowned slightly. "Weren't you hooked on that stuff? I don't think that would be wise, do you?" she asked.

"Hell no! I snorted heroin, not coke! And that, I promise, won't ever happen again, not ever!" Paula argued before Linda could respond. Paula continued. "Linda, I've been beaten, raped, peed on and not to mention I've eaten out of trash cans! I've been at my lowest!" Tears filled her eyes. Paula leaned face-to-face, eye-to-eye and nose-to-nose with Linda. "I'll die before another nigga take me through that hell again! Girl, look at me, this don't make no damn sense of how mature my body is, and I'm sitting here only 25 years old!"

Linda fell silent, deciding to not continue to protest her point. She allowed Paula to have her moment.

Paula could tell Linda felt her pain. Which meant, yeah, she did know something about Scotty's drug business! It was as if the girl was on at the Apollo Theatre and this was her opening night performance! A verse of Eminem's probed Paula's mind as she continued to perform her academy award winning role of word play to convince Linda hooking her up with some coke! Paula continued to rub Tiger, who snored in her lap. Linda glanced at the resting pup in Paula's lap. Tiger had never done that before. She decided to go with the good vibe she got from Paula. Besides that, there was no way she could live with the thought of turning Paula down and seeing her end up getting it from someone else and so happen to mishandle the package and the worst happen to her! Linda drew back a restless breath.

"Okay," she exhaled. "You win Paula; I know where the coke comes from."

"Duh, girl, do I look like I was born just yesterday? You can't slick a can of oil. I mean, look at you, Mrs. Lamborghini and mini mansion on an RN's salary!"

Linda laughed. "You got me. Well, my dad was Pablo Escobar's main guy in the U.S.!"

"Who?"

"Come here lil girl!" Linda led her into her library. It was large, with custom built book shelves on every wall. The tables were finished in red oak. The carpeting was a thick burgundy. Linda displayed several magazines out on the table and brought Paula up to speed. Linda laid the business down to her like she was a Special Forces Petty Officer! She wanted Paula to clearly understand that the dope game was an act of mental and physical war and there would always be causalities! For her to just endure the world's pain and learn to charge some things to the game and pay the hater back when she's bigger.

Paula's eyes bulged when it dawned on her that Pedro, Linda's father, was the actual leader of one of the most notorious drug trafficking rings in history, which was responsible for the distribution and sale of millions of kilos of cocaine around the world.

"So, Scotty worked for yo' old dude, huh?" Paula asked, looking up from the papers.

"Something like that," Linda said lowly. Linda left Paula seated alone at the table. She returned five minutes later and dropped a package on the table in front of Paula. "Scotty left that. Sell it and call me when it's sold." Linda then slouched onto the sofa beside Paula.

Paula grabbed the thick package and inspected it. "How much is it?" Paula wondered.

"I think it's a kilogram of coke." Linda pretended not to know. "I'm pretty sure it is!" she added.

"Damn, Lyn. What made you think I meant this much?" said Paula, examining the weight of the sealed vanilla package.

"Hey, I'm not going to be messing with that stuff! My days are long over and done. I'mma tell you this once, Paula, if you're not careful the temptation and immaterial desire for power and fame will someday come to unconsciously rule you and rob you of your true identity. Therefore, in a nutshell, I'm telling you baby girl, you got to take these drugs with their consequences and exactly how he left them. And if you get busted, please don't call ma house!"

Paula nodded yes.

"Oh, by the way, Scotty calls them sections! They weighed 1,008 grams; the cut measure is 252 grams per section."

"Fine, gim'me," said Paula and laughed as she stuffed the package into her purse. She went home and floated into her room and into thin air before dialing out to the stripper.

"Rough Business Escorts, how may I help you?" the secretary answered.

Paula booked a VIP date. She wanted the hottest entertainer. She requested for Mr. Pipe Dreams. An hour later, she glanced at her watch for the ninetieth time. "Where is this asshole?" she whined out loud. Then, it seemed only seconds later, the doorbell sounded through the hallway.

She sprinted through the house and snatched the door open and found him standing there, rocking a fitted T-shirt and skinny jeans. On his feet he wore flip flops and his hair was wet and hung loose. Paula grabbed him and literally drug him through the house.

"So, Mr. Pipe Dream, what is your name anyway?" she asked as she circled him.

He sat in a reclining chair in her bedroom. Paula had a blue steel Tarus .38 hair-trigger snub-nose that Linda had given her hidden under a Gucci pillow in case Pipe got the wrong idea.

He twisted his head, following her. "My name's Matt."

"Okay Matt. Remember our last convo about the pills and such?"

He sat up straight. "You found some already?"

"Better!" she opened the magazine she had stretched out on her dresser.

She told him to come look. He stood and walked to the dresser then looked down at the open mag. It revealed a pile of white powder smashed on a page.

His eyes lit up.

"Is it what I think it is?"

"Yeah. Try some."

Paula stepped back to allow him elbow room. He cut a window into the block, then produced his driver's license and began chopping the pile into finer particles. He then used the ID to make lines of powder. He pulled his leather wallet from his pocket and pulled out half of a straw, then leaned over the mag and placed the tip of the straw at the end of the line.

Paula watched him quickly inhale the coke as it disappeared into the straw.

He sniffed back the drugs into his nose and enjoyed the taste as it traveled down his throat. He coughed. His eyes quickly watered.

"Shit!" he exclaimed. He had a massive head rush. He stumbled as he reached for the chair. He found it and eased into it.

Paula sat Indian style on the edge of the bed in front of him. She smiled to see the immediate effect the coke took on him. Her shit had taken down Superman!

"I'm calling ma' shit kryptonite!" her mind bobbled.

"I'm like so high right now. I feel like I'm going crazy!" he said behind sniffing back more of the drug.

She nodded.

"Could I have some more?" he asked.

"Yeah, go ahead. Do you..." said Paula.

Matt went at another line.

"Hey, listen, I need someone trustworthy to help me sell it."

"Don't sweat it. That's only a rain drop to a river. I got chu!" he said before adding, "But we gone need someone like Worm to help me weigh and package it."

"What is a worm?" she asked.

"Not a what, a who! Worm is my youngest brother. That fool's like that with his numbers and the whip game."

'We gone make a fortune!' was all Paula thought about at that moment. Matt was just the brain she was looking for.

They rushed to see Worm. At their arrival in Sykeston, Missouri, only one hour outside of St. Louis, Paula looked surprised as Matt drove through a small patch of woods, then traveled down a dirt road. The trees ahead opened and let them into a large clearing. The house was opposite of Paula's expectation. She thought she was about to see an old run down farm boy's trailer with a Lassie type dog. Instead they had Bull Master Pits surrounding the spot.

Paula stared at a multi-level, traditional Century Hall Colonial home owned by Matt's grandparents, who lived in Miami. It was fabulous with a large pond behind it. They pulled into the four car garage. The moment Paula stepped outside the car, she heard loud music. A classic Plies CD, "100 years." Every beat was deafening.

Paula's eyes searched Matt's, who laughed.

"Oh, I forgot to tell you. Worm's mixed! I was adopted."

She followed him through the garage door. When they entered the house, a Lil Wayne track, Hustler Music from the Carter II album now pounded her chest. Paula placed her fingers into her ears. Matt went to the massive stereo system and set it to mute.

The vibe in the house was on chill. The light bulbs were dazzling over a beautiful aquarium that illuminated a fluorescent bright green light.

"Hey, brother Matt!" a feminine voice sounded.

Paula stared at the topless sista as she entered the room. She was built like an Amazon, standing over six feet tall. She had curves like Jennifer, from *Basketball Wives*. She was tatted just below her navel. Her flat abs sizzled. She wore only loose fitting white flamingo jeans standing pigeon toed and barefooted. Her toe nails were painted black, matching her fingernails.

"What's poppin' Tang? Where's your hubby?" Matt asked.

"In his own lil world and please don't make me say it." she responded.

Paula suspected them of fucking! There was no way a male stripper with a dick as huge as Matt's was ever going to withhold an exotic half naked diva pressing a perfect B cup on him and nothing happens! That was some BS to Paula!

"Who's she?" Tangy asked in her child like voice pointing at Paula.

"Friend of mine."

"So I guess you brought her to see the Wizard?" She laughed.

Matt smiled. It was an inside joke. Everybody who knew Worm called him the Wizard. People from all walks of the game used Worm's assistance. He was a complete nerd and a jack of all trades.

Tangy added, "Come on, follow me. You know he lives in his lil lab. So he stay on cloud nine!" Tangy sashayed in front of them. She stopped just at the entrance then footed aside.

"I can't go in there. I'm on na' punishment!" she stated and gestured them to enter.

The door had a large picture of a cloud and a purple number nine at the center. Paula frowned at Matt. She hated to see coward type men who took advantage of women. Matt hunched his shoulders as he entered. Clouds of thick smoke escaped the room. Paula coughed heavily while fanning smoke with her hand. "Jesus!" she gagged.

Matt went further though, leading the way. Paula blinked her eyes to adjust to the darkness and burning of the smoke. Her eyes finally adjusted.

The room was lit by a purple bulb. The atmosphere was like a trip on shrooms and Ex pills all in one. Worm sat thuggish on a long cotton sofa. In front of him sat a glass four hitter water filtered marijuana bongs that lingered with smoke. He sat topless, covered in hood tattoos. His arms had biblical sayings and numerous other pieces of art. His face had teardrops under his eyes. He was small like some stars when you see them in person. On his head was a St. Louis Rams fitted hat turned backwards. A 37 inch rose gold chain with a diamond snake medallion crossing his pectorals. His eyes were low. Paula thought they were shut.

"What it do lil' Bro?" said Matt.

"New hottie, huh?" Worm asked.

"Nah, she's here to see you, ma dude."

"So what's this adventure about?" Worm added, rubbing his knuckles greedily. He smiled.

Paula glanced at Matt and laughed. She took the lead though. Matt was beating around the bush.

"Look here. Let's skip all the pleasantries. Basically, can you help me shake a few ounces of blow?"

"You mean coke?" Worm asked.

"Yeah, whatever you want to name it."

She stuffed her hand into her large purse and aggressively snatched the package out. She sat it roughly on the table top. A small cloud of powder blew into the air. Worm immediately came to a sitting position on the couch and leaned forward.

"I know this ain't that shit!" He looked over to his brother in a sweat, who was nodding.

"Yes it is!"

Worm rubbed his fingers across the table and absorbed some of the spilled residue. He brushed it against his gums.

"Shit!" he stood, unable to feel his gums, or tongue. The room was Oval Office quiet. Worm invited himself to another line of the raw coke into his wide nostrils this time. The drug's potency hit him like a SCUD missile. This that Colombian flake!" Worm stated, brushing the back of his hand across his nose.

Paula was impressed, he liked it and knew exactly what it was, as Linda's face popped into her mind. She knew at this moment. Linda had blessed her and that she was at the right place to turn it into cash.

"Tangy!" Worm yelled.

She peeped her head through the doors keeping her feet hidden behind the threshold.

"Come in Bean, you off punishment." He glanced at Paula who was rolling her eyes at the crazy couple. "Don't hate the playa, hate the game, Lil Momma. She brought this on herself!" Worm noted in a raspy heroin voice.

"Man, how 'yo lil' butt gone put her on 'na punishment? Like you her daddy or something!" Paula hissed.

The fellas laughed brotherly.

Paula placed her right hand over her hip and raised her brows at Matt. "Really, she commented."

Matt's face became apologetic. Tangy loved that Paula stood up for her.

She smiled.

In defense, Worm shouted, "Tangy, why you laughing? Why don't you tell them what chu did, Ms. Innocent!"

Tangy sat beside Paula and folded her feet under her body batting her eyes innocently, her eyes probed the floor, then the ceiling before saying, "I got mad 'cause he was out of town and failed to call me, so I came down here and destroyed all of his precious glass weed pipes."

"So?"

She rolled her head at Worm, who looked surprised that she's grown nuts to stand up to him,. Tangy had smashed ten of his glass weed bongs into his grandmother's carpet. Paula raised her eyebrows and looked over to Tangy who bit at her nails while frowning babyishly. She hated that Worm put their personal business out there. In an ever so most innocent voice, she declared, "so you shouldn't have made me mad!"

"Yeah?" Worn boggled. "That's what chu on, huh?"

Tangy sealed her lips stained in Jennifer's bubble gum lip gloss defiantly.

"I can't ever believe you could actually fix yo damn trap to lie to yoself like you wasn't dead wrong."

"So what happen when you were stripping in Miami? Have I thrown that shit in yo face? Huh, do I?" said Worm three times.

"Snitch," Tangy murmured.

Paula elbowed her. "Try this," Paula requested.

Tangy made a line. She sniffed the coke and plopped onto the couch. She then smiled and crossed her legs. A soothing sense of horniness soaked between her legs. Good coke always made her coochie wet and her piece of man knew it.

"So is it wet?" he laughed.

She was still disappointed in him. She rolled her eyes. "Excuse me!" she left the room.

"This shit that deal! You feel me?" Worm added. "So what kind of plans you got cooking?" he asked Paula.

"Rock it up and of course, sell da shit! What else?" said Paula, tearing away at the paper wrapping.

"Wait, let me get my kite." He returned with a large box from under his mini bar. He emptied the contents on the table. A digital scale, a box of sandwich baggies, a box cutter razor, a circle mirror, and a pryex pot fell to the table. He then scooped 252 grams of B-12 from a dog food bag. He scattered his equipment all across the table. He weighed the kilo, whipped it, then broke it down into 54 ounces before breaking them into halves and quarter ounce bags.

Matt had left for a few seconds to see a client he hadn't seen in a while.

He quickly returned. Paula slept quietly at the foot of Worm's bed as he bagged the coke.

Nearly four hours later, Worm awoke Paula. She looked at the table top filled with different shaped plastic baggies of what seemed to be much more than her original kilo,

"What's all that?" she asked.

"I put Edward on that bitch!"

Paula just looked more confused.

"You know, Edward Scissorhands!" It's an expression niggas in the Boot Hills use when they put that whip on that dope.

"So what you put on it lil' bro?" Matt asked.

"I dry cooked 17 and spit on it with a spice of B-12 and this shit still some head buster. This how you make the real profit 'round here!"

"This shit's like early 60's gold! Now don't get it fucked up. This fuckin' white man's recession will destroy yo' ass if you don't buckle down to the powers that be and wait on yours. You'll end up crying victim and broke."

Worm preached as he lit a cigarette.

"Well, ma momma always told me when you live through someone else's ideas, you become their prisoner. And I must add, you only crawl on all fours because you haven't yet trained your mind to stand on yo' own two!" Paula explained. "So man up and quit bitching about what the white man has done and grab yo' nuts and take control of your own trailblazer! You are a king, black man and whitey ain't never played by his own rules! So remember power is taken, never given in this world. That damn shit died along with Brother Malcom X, fool! You feel me?" she said in closing.

Worm and Matt nodded, they understood.

So please be very clear on this so we won't have any altercations. "I want twenty racks off the muscle before any split.

"So you're saying, the extra change out of the pot, we'll split three ways, huh?" Worm asked. She nodded yes. He went on explaining the whip game to her.

Paula gave Matt twenty ounces and worm 30 ounces to flip from his spot. "Now be mindful fellas, Any shorts will come out of your end of the split, or y'all asses!"

Soon after, Matt dropped her off at approximately 11:00pm, back in Hustle City. She awoke the next day to the sound of robins chirping. They were scattered throughout a bush beneath her window just open. She wiggled her small feet into her Tasmanian slippers, then showered and had a light breakfast of bagels and eggs.

Diamond had long before been up and gone to work. Paula's Galaxy 6 phone sounded at 9:32am. She hardly recognized the number.

She answered, "Hello?"

"What it do Nipps?" Worm giggled at the nickname he'd giver Paula. Nipps was short for Nipples. Her nipples were excessively noticeable when she wore soft bras and thin blouses.

"Who is this?" she demanded with an attitude.

"Think it's a game!" he teased playfully.

"Worm! What's up, Crazy?"

"I need you to slide out to Cape Girardeau. We got a situation with them clothes you dropped off for my girl."

She disconnected and raced, disregarding the girl time her and Diamond had planned. She had a million and five disastrous thoughts storming her brain.

She searched the kitchen for the keys to the beamer, Diamond had given her.

Paula had misplaced them. There was no time for her to go searching, but she had no choice. Then she found them and rushed to the car. She turned the gold key in the ignition. The engine came alive. Paula pulled Diamond's Khole sunglasses from the sun visor and placed them over her natural silky face. It was aggravating with dry heat, luckily, she drove in A/C.

Paula soon arrived at Worm's location. Her small diamond clustered fist hammered the glass door, she wore short shorts and pink and white flip flops. Tangy answered quickly, wearing a terrycloth robe.

"Hey Pauli, come on in girl!"

Paula narrowed her eyes at Tangy who looked a hot mess. Tangy's hair was still neatly managed, but her face looked worn out. The bags under her eyes were deep and her eyes were huge like headlights.

"Let me guess, y'all been up getting high all night?" Paula questioned the couple.

Worm was slouched on his comforter pillow playing (Lil' Wayne *How da Love* in his PJ's and Cartier glasses. "Something like that," he answered. "Tangy; bring it!" he shouted.

Tangy disappeared into the house and Paula stood with her hand on her wide hip frowning at Worm. His ego reminded her too much of Peter. "Please, tell me you motherfuckers did not fuck up ma shit!" Paula screamed.

Tangy returned at Worm's next call. She handed Paula an envelope.

She opened it. "Holy shit!" she exclaimed. "Is this everything?"

"That's yo' eight stacks and I kept fo' bucks of the profit like you said."

Tangy laid beside him as he fired up a blunt filled with Purple Kush.

Paula studiously thumbed through the cash. "N'all. I said split after I get my 20 G's!" Then we'll do the three way splitting!" she added. "So nigga, you could unass the rest of my Paypa!" She placed her hand into her Alexander McQueen purse.

He sent Tangy for Paula's other $8,000. She hit his hand with a few hundred on G.P.

"Cool!" he honored.

"How did you sell it all in just a matter of hours?" she asked,

"If I tell you, I'll have to kill you." They laughed,

Tangy spoke out, "girl, once a few of them geeks tried it, it was a story that told itself!" she puffed away at the cigar, "I got some mo' Paypa waiting as we speak, so you need to be handing me some more work!"

"You dig?" said Worm.

Paula raced home and took them 20 ounces this time. Worm sat at the kitchen table with two anonymous burnout phones in front of him. Paula sat across from him fumbling through a tabloid magazine. She loved to read up on White folk's drama.

Tangy lay relaxed on the sofa answering her old dancing friends from Miami Tweets.

The tiny phone vibrated. "Yo, I'm on my way."

No sooner did he end one call, others continued to buzz for the coke. Worm was still on line with a customer that wanted two and a baby (two ounces and a quarter).

Paula answered worm's calls. "What's up?" she whispered,

"Where's Worm?"

"He busy at the moment, what chu need?"

The caller hesitated.

"Look here, call back then!" Paula bluffed to hang up. Being that she walked in the caller's shoes at one point, she knew the pull of an addiction.

"OK, I need a ball!"

"Who dis?" she asked.

"Stanley!"

"Hey, Stan, this is Worm sister, China. Come on through. I got chu!" she told the drug craved man. "Oh, and Stan, I don't have a car, so if you want this blessing I have for you, you'll have to come see me. You better hurry because it's almost gone," she lied.

"I'll be there in three minutes. I guess I could steal ma sister's ride!

Don't sell ma package!" Stan begged.

Worm listened to her handle pesty Stan. He decided that while she was there, she should answer calls.

"OK, but there's one issue. The ones without rides you would have to deliver. "Deal?" she asked.

"Of course," said Worm.

Stan came skidding to the curb. He purchased his ball for $70.

"Damn, I thought you were gon' bless me!" said Stan, gaming.

"Man, get cha crazy ass out of here!" Paula replied before handing him three additional tenths of coke.

Stan smiled.

"Let me know if you need to rent the car, China," he added sitting into his sister's 2010 Nissan Leaf.

Paula pitied him. "No thank you, Stan!" she closed the door.

As the day unfolded, the crazier shit became. Worm and Tangy were both out making separate deliveries while Paula attended the following door sales. Paula was well schooled. She took care of business fiercely. She was there alone with her only friend in her hand at all times; her trusty 380. She paid attention to every detail.

As the day progressed, she hadn't caught a moment to search through her Kindle Fire for a print-on-demand best seller novel published and written by Darrell Wells, *Snitch Factor Rule #35.*

Tangy noticed Paula was a natural at scheming custos and could make them feel blessed at the same time. Other hustlers and hypes became spoiled and began to run game for more dope. Paula would thumb her nail through all the plastic and break the chunks down four ways and hand them from the same package. They thanked her for blessing them. She was diligent to her crew. Without any contact from Hustle City, Paula kept all of her drugs in a motel in West Cape Girardeau. Her and the people she now called family, got it in for two weeks of raw grinding. At the rate they were rolling, the inevitable happened. They ran out of coke!

"Damn it," Paula whimpered. She realized selling it and being unable to keep up was identical to the sickness users have during a drought season.

She sat alone in her motel room browsing names who she thought had or knew someone with the shit to no avail. Everyone she recalled dogged her during her days of using. With her remaining breath, she called Linda's cell in distress.

"Sugar, I need you so like desperately!" said Paula.

"What is it Boo?" Linda returned.

"I need you to meet me at your spot like yesterday!"

"I'm here now, but I got to be at work in the next hour or so, though that evil hoe, Diamond, been riding a bitch ass lately! Oh, speaking of her, she asked me have I saw you. Don't worry, I told her you were helping me on some things. I reckon she blind to the fact you out in these streets again, huh?" Linda guessed.

"I'll tell her some day, but right now, I'm like 2 hours out of the city.

So I'll see you when you get off work, ok?" said Paula.

Paula raced down Highway 70 East like a mother in labor. Later that night, she gladly parked beside Linda's truck. She ran up the stairway with her wedge sandals in hand. Linda watched from her home surveillance camera.

"I need more now. Lyn!" she whined, bursting into the unlocked door.

Linda locked eyes with her closely. She didn't look as if she were using, despite her odd, exhausted look. Linda knew that look, but couldn't quite place it. "What's up, hot girl?"

As Linda released their hug, Paula answered by emptying her large rainbow colored Carrolyn Carter bag on the Pergo wood table. It was much more than Linda's money she owed.

"Damn bitch! Yo ass working with them people, or something?" asked Linda jokingly. "No, for real girl! How did you make this money this damn fast?" she asked as she counted the big face bills.

"You can't change a leopard's spots! Once a cheetah always a cheetah!" Paula smiled.

Linda had counted millions in her time.

"So what could I score for twenty of that?"

Linda disappeared as usual. She returned five minutes later carrying a Britney Spears (Spears for Sears) shopping bag by its string. She sat the bag onto her glass table in front of Paula, who found the moment to search her Black & Yellow Kindle for the book True Dawgs Diamond asked of her. Paula leaned over the bag. It was three kilograms on top of a pair of Pajama Jeans.

Linda tossed her middle finger to Paula. They laughed. Paula blinked at the package as she moved towards Linda.

"You sneaky bitch! You had these all along!"

"Yeah, but I had to be sure you weren't going to smoke them up, Smoky!"

Linda teased.

"Aw, we got addict jokes now, huh?"

Linda rolled her eyes with a smile. "I"m just sayin'," she added, jerking her body back.

"Bitch, how much I owe you now?" Paula wanted to know.

Linda sipped from her drink. "Ten thousand dollars. Daddy sold them to Scotty for six thousand each. Little did either of them know, was that those prices were given for someone purchasing shipments of 1,000 kilos or better. It was the only time prices decrease. Linda was just glad to be getting her home rid of the drugs she found clearing out Scotty's storage in Los Angeles, California.

Paula took two of the kilos home where she continued to play the helpless victim. She soon returned to the Boot Hill with only one kilo. Together they cut, bagged and weighed it. This time, they bagged 33 individual bags of circles and 30 of half circles. The remaining 6 ounces went into grams and 8 balls. Paula disfavored putting a lot of cut on the work, which Worm suggested.

"Look, I don't wanna use that much cut anymore. The better it is, the faster we'll sell it!" spoken like a true madam.

She proved to be right.

Instead of cutting the work with another nine ounces of B12 supplements, her cocaine was at least 83% pure Colombian flake. Worm only used what she suggested. The coke was still fire. In fact, so fire that Worm began receiving calls from customers that were admitted to the hospital for signs of overdosing. The minute their eyes would open feeling better, they would call Worm and inform him of why they haven't been through. They ended each call with the same last words each time. "I'll be through as soon as I get discharged."

Lucky for Paula, her safe house was located in a secluded area, West of Cape Girardeau, Missouri. Cape being as small as it is, everyone knew your business fast.

Matt was selling more coke at the gym than the places sold protein shakes.

All the trainers and escort's colleagues hit him when their dates and people wanted cocaine powder.

Paula ran through the three packages within the same two weeks it took to move then the first one. Linda was awestruck. She always warned Paula to check her workers back ground.

"Paperwork!" her mind tumbled. Paula watched these people sell the coke; therefore, they were a 100 in her book! Linda gave her another three bricks.

"Ok Pauli, on my life these are the last of them and as much as I'm enjoying yo' money, you're gonna have to find a new connect."

Paula took the drugs and felt disappointed of the news Lyn hit her with.

This time, the three kilos seemed like she never had them. They were gone by the following Friday. She showed back up at Linda's door without a purse this time.

It was all hugs like normal. The divas chattered about girl stuff and played through a few hands of the card game, Casion.

"Well Lyn, I must be honest. I've searched my brain with a fine tooth comb for someone and still there's nothing' How about Scotty?"

Linda palmed her forehead. "Honey, I do not feel like digging up those bones; my life has moved on!"

"Ok, how about you take me to see Scotty?" Paula was desperate.

"What? No, I'm not going to that place!" She promised herself that she would never see him caged in like some animal. She had a TV version of prison. Steel bars, homosexuals and stabbings.

"Well, can I get his address?" Paula asked.

"Now that, I can do," said Linda as she walked through the house followed by Paula. She kneeled and relaxed her knee into the plush carpet. She pulled the bottom drawer out and fumbled through some old letters. "Here it is!" she mumbled as she retrieved the letter with the blank visiting form inside. Scotty had sent it to her months ago, but she didn't do jails, nor prison time with men. It was an emotional rollercoaster she'd rather miss. She handed the letter to Paula. "Good luck! The rest is up to you, Doll! And remember, dealing with his kind is a gamble, but I understand you got to do what chu got to do!"

Paula had no idea where Linda was headed with that statement.

Linda knew if Scotty agreed to continue any form of business with someone as beautiful, young and naive as Paula, that it meant he'd gotten that pussy; she knew the freak in him. "There's an empty visiting form inside," said Linda poutily.

Paula opened the envelope. She rushed home to fill it out correctly, then her and Diamond sat on the sofa watching their favorite TV show, (Scandal). They tried to enjoy every spare moment together though Diamond was on call 24/7.

When Diamond went to her room, Paula filled out the visiting form. She lied on the application about her relation with Scotty, saying that she was Scotty's sister from out of town. The next morning, she stopped by the post office and mailed it.

Scotty slipped on his Nike shower shoes and stumbled out the door. His celly laughed as he looked down the walkway, while placing his feet into his own flip flops. He walked into the C.O.'s office to receive his mail; the C.O. had shouted his name just moments ago.

"Mayors!" said Scotty.

The officer handed him the folded paper. He walked away, ripping it open.

He couldn't wait. He suddenly stopped in his tracks at the acceptance of a visitor's request form.

"Paula?" he whispered, confused. "I don't know no damn Paula!" he returned to his cell and pulled up a chair. His only mail was coming from several land marks outside of the U.S. Besides that, he enjoyed reading up on the sexy hot divas of KYTE cuties online from his hook (secret cell phone.)

"I have no clue who this could be." He hoped it was Hoops. He facebooked her often, he noted to his celly (Wise).

"Shidd!" Wise added.

Scotty crashed back onto his bunk and tucked his huge head in deep thought, staring at the ceiling. He figured it must have been another fancy move of the DA's advance to pursue him to testify. He'd already turned them down several times before. He stuck to the code.

That Friday it was hot and humid. Paula dressed in a conservative Dereon from fitting blouse and hip hugging Penny Brown (Zyion jeans.) She leaned against her new Mercedes, her Zyion big face shades were pulled just above her forehead, mirroring her sexy hot pink painted toes wrapped in Gucci Stilettos as she glanced at them. Snapping a shot at them from her Galaxy cell. Her long hair fell neatly down her back. She walked into the Jennings Federal holdover facility. The officers hassled her for not being approved on his list. Paula told them she was from out of town and more than anything wanted to see her older brother. That someone had passed away in their family.

A female officer searched and warned her with a freakish look at Paula's ass as she headed through the metal detector and signed in at the desk.

She then sat inside a cubicle. The Male guards stared at her thirstily as Scotty entered on the opposite side of the booth dressed in an orange jump suit. A 6'2" guard stood over Scotty. Scotty stared at Paula as if her head was about to do a 360° twist.

Paula exhibited no signs of nervousness. She looked up. Her sweet faced dazzled him and the guards, mirroring his first wife. She was 26 at the time and very mature. She placed her hand into Scotty's lap as he had done hers. She slid a little closer to feel his presence,

"Are we being recorded?" she asked softly. "Could they hear us? she asked.

Scotty's head quickly signaled no. "Don't I know you?" he asked.

120

"No. I'm a true BFF of Linda's."

Scotty reclined into his seat, frowning at the mention of Linda's name.

She was now officially on his shit list. He removed her from his Corrlinks Email and visitation list. Paula's face adjusted for him to at least hear her reason for being there.

He obeyed like a puppy.

"Look, fuck what you and ma bitch have cooking undone," she stated, seemingly desperate. "Beside everything, it's just as much of your fault as hers. You should have known whenever the husband gets busted, wifey takes it all, especially being Lyn isn't the type to ride out prison bid with anyone. Definitely after that Saint Tropez stunt Yo'ass pulled on her! Dude, keep it real," she furthered, Paula spoke of the last trip he and Linda experienced, which was as ugly as ever.

Where Scotty had admitted to making out with a supermodel the second night they docked the rented fifty foot Mercedes yacht. That day lived to be the highlight of their divorce.

"After all, Scotty, we both know she's not from the world you and I come from, being

her father sheltered and spoiled her." She was on a roll. "Like I said, I'm not here to remind you of a pill you swallowed long ago."

"Well, what are you here for?" he asked.

"Business. What else is there?" She added. "I took care of those little problems you left at Linda's. As a matter of fact, all seven of them and now that they're all gone, I wanna keep solving your girl's problems. But the magic question is, can you assist me?" All what Paula had said was on point. She was indeed who she claimed to be. He caught the gist. Linda had sent her for his connection, meaning she had found his hidden drug kitty.

"I like you." was all he said.

Paula smiled. "Have you read the ten commandments?" she asked.

Scotty nodded yes. It was an agreement that he'd just agreed to her prices at $10K each. "Done," said Scotty.

Paula brushed a single strand of hair from her forehead. "Fine." She winked at him.

He gave her a number to call the following day. She left the jail and drove downtown to the Court Yard Hotel. She crashed the moment she touched the soft bed. The sun rose the next morning. And so did Paula. Hours seemed to have dragged. By 6:00am, 6:42am, 7:00am, 7:37am. At 8:25am, she left the hotel to revisit Scotty. Scotty eased into his seat. "Look under the table," he spoke.

She discreetly fondled under her end of the table. She felt a small piece of paper taped to the bottom. She removed it and quickly slid it into her bra. "On the tenth commandment, how do you want me to do it?" she inquired of the transaction of the money.

"I'll send you an offshore account number," he replied.

Paula kept her voice soft and low. "Done. I'll handle it ASAP."

She waved goodbye as she exited the visiting room. Scotty saw dollar signs like a winning lottery ticket in her eyes. "That's one hot piece of ass." he pondered.

Paula walked out into the beaming sunlight. She got into her rental car and removed the piece of paper from her bra. It read, Monday storage: 252-599-2016 PS code word: 99.

Paula was scared. She knew she was stepping into a dangerous lifestyle which meant her dealing with some dangerous people. She decided she was ready for that challenge. She called the number that same evening. She cracked her window for some air.

"Hello?" a deep voice with a Cuban accent answered.

"My name is..."

"Stop. No names, sweetheart," the voice interrupted her. "Code numbers only."

"99," Paula whispered.

The line disconnected. She stared at her Galaxy phone. Within seconds a text came through. It read. 702 Marris Lane, Cubar Hill West Indies. Friday morning. Do not be late!

Friday morning, Paula drove to Lambert Airport and boarded the flight she had booked from her smart phone. The stewardess greeted her with a friendly smile. She ordere a drink to enjoy her ten hour flight in first class. She sipped on a Call-lá-cab cocktail until she fell asleep. She awoke feeling a bit hung just as the plane touched down.

The international flight 157 US Corporate G-6 jet landed at a private gate #11 on schedule. The staff steered passengers out after the ground crew adjusted the steps.

Paula caught a taxi cab to her hotel that sat west, beyond dirt roads and hills that were almost completely deserted. Her nerves were racing. She had forty eight stacks in her luggage. She was dressed in a Royal brilliant blue shoulderless Khloe Dash sundress. She felt half naked for the occasion. The area was covered in coconut palm trees. Two black Land Rovers seated three white suited large men with dark Aviator sunglasses and straw boater hats. It was either her people, or them people. Either one, she was still spooked.

As she watched the traffic from her 7th floor casino window, two pearl white Honda FC hybrid sport coupes pulled onto the hotel's narrow cobblestone street beside the Rova's. The streets were empty. The air was dry and hot.

For the comfort of company she ordered a steak and fry dish. The waitress served her and continued onto her duties.

Paula stopped the lady. "Can you please tell me anything about this hotel? I mean, I've tried to pull it up on Map Quest, but it doesn't show."

The lady spoke in a sneaky voice. "Young lady, you should watch yourself talking to strangers in strange lands." She smiled and moved on.

The hotel was owned by Scotty's connect. Moments later, her room door opened and closed quickly. There stood a guy who favored Lopez late night. Paula's fingers tightened over her steak knife as she stood. "Excuse me! What are you doing here? This room's taken! I have a gun!" she lied in fear.

"Hold it my lady. I'm #99," he shouted across the room. Her connect had arrived.

Paula sat and waved him closer in relief. "So what's with me making such long risky travel for only a few kilos?" she asked.

He sipped down the rest of Paula's drink only to taste the sweetness of her lip stick from her glass, he then made a sudden phone call, spoken in a fluent Spanish. "Ok, my lady, your package is ready. You may reschedule your flight to the States."

"Oh, I only called you out here to see you in person. Scotty bragged of your beauty," he added. "I had to see if the old chap still had that eye and as for the White Diamonds, they're at this address." The man tapped the address into her cell. The location was a small storage bin in South St. Louis that sat off Broadway.

Paula decided to spend the rest of her evening having hot sympathy sex with a total stranger next door. who had been eye balling her from the minute she stepped out of the spa area in a silk Cookie Johnson's wraparound, fitting over her matching two piece bikini set she brought along to make this an official vacation/business adventure before she headed out the following night. She planned to make it home in time to beat the bothersome crowd at the Western Union where she routinely sent her mother Pam $400 Quick Collect monthly for prison hygiene and commissary spending. She had fun with the girls the following weekend, secretly building her drug empire before she headed out to the projects to reunited with her uncle James.

CHAPTER TWELVE – 1-4
Weebies

Paula paused for a moment inspecting her surroundings before continuing down the murky hallway inside the dimly lit building. It was one of the high rises left in south downtown.

Paula being led by her old addict instincts moved sporadically, quietly scanning the group of Blood gang members kneeled at the end of the hall where the only light was cast from C.K. man, Dead Head and a mix-breed female named Ree Ree. The group all stood on post Paula made no eye contact with them. They questioned her presence on sight.

"Aaa bitch! Who the fuck you looking for?" someone shouted.

"How much you spending?" Ree Ree added.

"It's right here!" they competed.

"N'all I'm straight," Paula answered.

The sun faded away as the entrance door closed behind her. Her, My Life perfume lingered throughout the tiny hall. Her hair was pulled into a pony tail.

She covered and checked her watch as she waited for the elevator. It came.

She pinched her nose to blur the breathtaking aroma of urine that fouled the small elevator.

The elevator shook as it ascended. It stopped on the 7th floor. At this point, Paula had been back from her trip for two weeks and now contemplated the trip she made the day she returned to Worm's. She had estimated that Worm and Matt couldn't sell the quantity of cocaine she would need sold. She thought back to the day She Last spoke to worm.

"No way...no how."

"I could do at best 2 kilos a week," Worm claimed.

Paula had returned with 25 bricks. They were sold to her at 6,000 each with her owing the Colombians 150,000 dollars, which was nothing to her.

"That's not what I had in mind, Worm," she added.

"So what was you expecting?"

"Like five or six each."

"Woman, you crazy as hell. We'll have to sell dat shit by big eights only.

Is that what chu expect a nigga to do?" he asked as Paula rocked and grooved to her shit by Magale playing from Tangy's iPod.

Worm continued, "I mean, don't forget, you ain't Ms. Scarface in those stilettos and I'm damn sho ain't no Mathano. So let's get this shit straight!"

Matt hurried to clean up Worm's comment. "Yeah Paula, the kid has a valid point."

"I don't give a fuck about his point, just get mine to the house!" she swore, gazing over the ten kilos lying on Worm's lap as she left them to handle their business. She knew in order to possibly sell the amount of bricks like Scotty, she'd have to use every inch of advice Linda had armed her with and surely a lot of good people would be hurt at the end of the day. On that note, she had to spread her hustle ties. It was time for her to return to the very death infected streets that had once taken everything she loved and nearly her own life as well.

"It will either free me of my pain or serve me a quick death." Paula had put that on her mother's life, which is how she ended up in the hallways of the Webbies Projects.

At that very instant, Paula was more than willing to wrangle with the game's deepest depths. That the real money and street cred laid at the heart of the inner city.

Her reason for being in the center of those projects was to assure her protection. She would face all of her fears once again. Although much had changed, she had sworn to eat the weak and bury her losses.

She knocked at the door of the last piece of family she had left despite of his habitual heroin addiction. She wanted someone of genuine blood behind her holding the gun that guarded her life. That person was James, her father's youngest brother and her favorite uncle, even though her mother had forbidden him from seeing Paula.

The moment Paula was old enough he had sent for her and had her brought to his project apartment. She could hardly remember the first time she saw his evil side. She was 16 years old. Her so called lil' boyfriend at the time was highly jealous. Styles was his name. When she had grown tired of his whorish ways and claimed their break up official, he had stolen her purse.

He had lightweight robbed Paula of her down payment for her first used car.

Paula had worked all summer at Sonic for that money.

She now smiled, but had buckets of tears when her uncle James spoke to her about it then. He was always dressed in Jack Boy gear and and drove only old school cars.

None of that mattered to the young ladies as long as he was a sweetheart to her. That day, he drove circling Style's block. Just so happened Styles pulled up in a wild cherry Chrysler 300. He bought it after he'd flipped her hard earned money. She cried not only because he took her cash, but because she still loved the ungrateful bastard. It was almost 7:15pm. He stepped out of the 300 as Uncle James piss gold '76 Seville drove up.

"That's him!" Paula pointed.

James double parked. "Sit tight precious."

The sun was at set. James cut into Styles out of nowhere and fired a volley of rounds at him. Styles was hit once in his rib cage. The moment he hit the pavement, U.J. went into his pockets and emptied them. He calmly returned to his car. "Here, baby girl. You want me to kill that lil' nigga?"

Paula cried, shaking her head 'no'. She knew that her uncle was throw'd off. She remembered that day and smiled as she knocked harder.

She wore tight black Sex Code blue jeans, a pair of number 4 red and black Jays and a red and black ball cap. Her long hair was drawn into a ponytail and hung through the fitting loop. She banged on the worn out door at the sight of one of the dudes approaching her direction. The hallway tiled flooring was heavily cracked like boiled eggs. She knocked rapidly, her knuckles hurting.

"Yeah!" The voice yelled from inside the door.

She crossed her arms at the moment, feeling tension of old boy that was now two doors away. He was obviously checking her to see if she had anything worth robbing her for. Luckily, she had thought to hide those long thick legs, shapely hips and plump ass in some normal fitting clothes. She was smart. She declined to wear her jewelry out showing. She wore a Sponge Bob book bag with a kilo of cocaine hidden in it.

"Eh, home girl. What's yo name?" he asked. At the second he looked into her bold eyes, he knew she wasn't there to cop drugs. Her eyes were pure white, her scent was tasteful. Everything she had on was new. She never took her keen eye off of him.

"You wanna hit this blunt, Shawty?" he asked.

"No thank you." It was nice that he asked, she thought.

Suddenly a sleep filled voice approached the other side of the door.

"Who is it?" U.J. asked.

He couldn't make out her face. She wore the ball cap drawn over her forehead.

"Pauuula!" She yelled in a rushful tone. "Open the door, uncle. It's me!"

He opened it and was glad to see her face. Old boy gazed her as she entered.

The condition of James' front room was pitiful. She saw lumps of bed linen scattering the floor. A mumble and movement sounded from one of the piles that smelled like old laundry.

"Hey! Man, close those damn blinds! A motherfucker trying to sleep!" A voice yelled.

Paula's eyes adjusted to the room's new lighting. It was like a ray from God on their situation. Paula made her lil' stank face.

"Who are these people?" she asked softly.

"None of yo' damn business lil' nosey ass girl!" her uncle replied, pulling her into his unslept-in bedroom. The tiny room was kept neat.

"I miss you uncle!" she hugged him.

"Yeah, I guess that's why you let that lil' nigga disrespect this family, huh?" James stated. "The only reason he still breathing is because of you.

And that I can promise you, it won't happen again and that shit's on my nephew Sammie!" He'd always swore on Johnny, AKA Sammie, Paula's father when he was pissed.

"I wish you would have murked that nasty dick bastard. He burnt me twice and acted like he never knew me when I saw him at Club Rolex a few summers back," she lied for the sake of conversation. She knew James enjoyed drama.

Styles had also ganked her on a drug deal and made her give him sex in a gangway on D.S.T. (Desoto) street.

Paula stepped over to the window. She stayed put as she began searching the thoughts of her past life tales from the beginning of her dropping out of VAP, an all girl's vocational school. She talked for what seemed like hours nonstop. Uncle James simply nodded at certain aspects. He had that junkies itch. He felt her pain and grieved over her sad tragedies. Mostly he was proud of his choice to let her go out on her own and find her own way in life. Despite all she would face, she was still alive and ever so beautiful.

It warmed his heart to see someone so young go out in the storms of that merciless world, so feeble and alone and find the strength to break through a situation that still haunted him. Paula never forgot where she came from.

James patted her shoulders. "You are definitely John's daughter, with yo' momma's features."

"I guess I have my uncle's habits, huh?" Paula teased.

Now it was his turn to catch her up on his life. As she could see, he still carried that monstrous heroin habit. His children were scattered around the country by different users and sober school teachers. He'd been up to the same ole same ole trying to feed that monkey on his back that had an infinite appetite. Lately, he had hooked up with three fellow addicts that slept in his front room. They had been doing paper bank robberies and petty licks in the 3700 block of California. It was what they became respected for throughout the projects. They used junkies from other hoods to rob late night hustlers who were caught with their pants down throughout the P.J.'s. They were the worst kind of dope fiends to come across.

They barred none!

They were pushing niggas shit back for a little bit of nothing! She narrowed her eyes at him when he mentioned that their last job was a bank. He confessed that they planned to rob another bank the following day. She stared, annoyed at him.

The whole idea was so foolish to her. She had no idea anyone could get so much prison time for five punk ass grams of crack cocaine than he would doing bank jobs without using any weapon. And to think they'd found her loving mother guilty for killing to save her two innocent daughters.

"How much ya'll ever got on one job?" she asked.

"About eight grand," he said as if it were a lot of money.

"Really!" she sassed with her palms over her wide hips. "So your plan is to keep running up in banks, passing stupid notes for a measly eight G's?" she asked.

"Ain't no question! huh, man!" he chuckled.

"I got a better idea," said Paula, lying across his bed with her legs crossed.

He laughed. "Like what?" he asked. "You know dick don't sell like pussy these days."

She ran it down to him then stared at him seriously.

"I mean, what do you know about cocaine, Paula?" he asked.

"Don't play with me like that!" she says. Paula hated to be patronized.

"A'ight, baby girl! What's ya plan?" He wanted to know.

"Step one is to clean up this pig pen and put those bums in there to some real use and make some real money."

"That's all?" he asked, scratching his head.

"Yeah. Plus the kilo of coke I brought with me to start us off." She smiled, tossing the package at James' bare feet.

"Is that enough?" she said.

"You better know it!" he agreed.

Paula sat the entire evening with two things she hoped to acquire. A handful of goons and a point of home base operation.

Uncle James wasted no time at all. The moment he agreed, she tore open the kilo at his feet. He gathered his crew. The four men and Paula sat at the kitchen round table breaking it down to street level quantity.

Paula sat beside James in a mental elaborate party, chatting on Facebook with a male friend from her seventh grade class who've had had a crush on her.

At the same time, she observed every package. James cut and the others bagged. She thought of his guys, her uncle's age. Wayne was light skinned and tall, like a basketball player. He was obviously the ladies man of the crew with his freshly flat ironed slacks and silk shirt. Uncle Shugg was the oldest at 42. His hair was curly and he had huge intimidating arms. Uncle J was the youngest at 37. He was a large man weighing 246 pounds. They had the entire table covered. James planned to stop using.

It was almost six in the evening when Paula followed them into the courtyard in front of their building where they advertised that they had quarters, half and whole ounces of crack at what was nowadays considered as highway prices. $150/$250/$500...each. They moved around the building and various cuts throughout the projects most of the night.

Paula stayed posted inside guarded by Coop. She relaxed like a queen on the now Febreeze-smelling couch reading a Knemiziz publication novel, *Monster Goddess*. Diamond turned her onto reading urban works.

Later, Paula made a series of moves back and forth dropping off money. She spent some time on the balcony watching Wayne and James making hand to hand sales. It surprised her. They were so on point and cautions of who they sold to. Dudes that had candy painted whips were now copping their drugs from her. Coop was Paula's designated bodyguard. He wasn't a heroin junkie. His choice was that purple kush weed and the thrill to kill.

"You on ma nieces detail twenty-four hours a day regardless of what she say!" James told him.

The first couple of months went as sweet as momma's Kool-Aid on a scorching hot summer day. Paula's Paypa was stacking high, but the day came when the guys from other parts of the projects felt they weren't eating like they were supposed to. The heroin-heads were doing far too much! Paula's uncle's had still used, but they stayed focused with their portion of Paula's coke business. The 1-4 Project building was booming. The once car thieves and bank robbers became major eight ball distributors, riding cash paid for Challengers on deuces.

Uncle James had purchased a two story home for his elder sister in Walnut Park on Beacon next door to Chingy's mother's house. He had also copped a black cherry '69 convertible Bonneville on solid gold, 24 inch hundred spoke bullet Daytons.

The more money they raked in, the more armor and heavier artillery they had to arm those who were obviously now on Paula's payroll. She had a sentry of authority at every exit and entry.

Back in the Boot Hills, Worm had begun putting more cut on the dope and pocketing the extra loot. His numbers stayed the same. No one in the Boot Hill could match his low prices of $700 a zip. He had the big head and Tangy hated it. She had to listen to all the rumors of him sleeping with ho's that once wouldn't have stood close to him. His operation was a maze without Paula standing over him.

Paula's time was now preoccupied back in the Lou, literally controlling the P.J.'s. Her Boot Hill operation now became secondary. Therefore, Matt found no reason to go that way. Worm had become a total asshole.

Paula was ripping and running so much, she wrestled with making a moment to actually count all of her money together. Her money was buried in her Mercedes trunk, under Linda's dog house, that Tiger never slept in and as an extra safety net, she stashed it in several safe deposit boxes and trust fund accounts. Her paper was everywhere other than her spot.

Friday night, she gladly gathered all of her cash under one roof. As she counted the stacks covered her bedroom. She had piles of hundreds on the bed, on top of the dresser, falling out of her huge purse. Finding it hard to breathe, her heart trembled in her chest! After her count, she had an unbelievable $1.5 million and some charge in cash counting the sixteen ounces Worm played around with, secretly re-upping coke from an outside connect located in Sikeson, Missouri. The system she put together was brilliant.

Uncle James schooled Paula. She proved to be an intelligent student despite her sometimes controlling ways, James thought. She was so detailed. She now stood at the top of the same game, from the inside looking out, that had once completely broken her inside and had no idea of how to fix it.

Paula followed Coop, who wore a bulletproof vest and carried a black and chrome state trooper's 40 Glock. He keyed his way into their trap spot.

Paula smiled as she admired James' new outfit. He wore a lime green/black three piece suit over some Jolly Rancher colored Gators.

"Guess we need to get something on point," said Paula.

They quickly seated at the round table. "I'm very much thinking we could stand to make a lot more money if we get rid of those dudes in the parking lot. They're blocking my money!" she said.

This was true. Bel-Bel, his MOB, Lil' Greasy and them had been hustling on the lot in front of 1-4 high rise for going on a month now. Their sole reason was to catch the weight customers before they entered the building to buy from Paula. Now, Paula was pissed!

The crud-ball move they were making was costing her bi-weekly an decrease of 30 to 45 thousand bucks. The money wasn't her big issue. The young renegades were disrespectful and had not gotten her approval. Considering her options, she decided to get the sale blockers relocated back to the 4200 block of West Bell Ave.

"I want them out of our way!" said the queen.

James nodded in agreement.

About one hour later, approximately 6:27pm the same day, three masked armed jack boys invaded the parking lot of the eight story high rise located on 14th and Chodoe Ave. The trio of stick men exited a rented Chevy Impala.

They confronted Bel-Bel and a couple of his guys. The jack boys were armed with Choppa's AK-47 rifles. The youngsters were taken by surprise and stripped of their valuables. After the gunmen made the boys drop it like it's hot! The tall masked man stepped forward and aimed his AK at Bel-Bel and shot him in the eye. The blast knocked him off his feet. His body then hugged the pavement like dry paint. The robbers fled as the boy's blood pooled around his head. He died at the cause of living the code of being a real nigga. They say, "What you live by, you die by!" Thus, leaving those you swore to love to bear the burden of your death is far worse than pleading at the feet of your enemies. For young souls like lil' Bel-Bel, his million dollar move turned out to be a two dollar finish. He was pronounced DOA at St. Joseph's Hospital two weeks before his twenty-first birthday. Paula never meant for the boys to be killed. It was supposed to be a bluff tactic to remove them. Bel-Bel bucked, therefore, Coop had no choice but to serve him steel. The next day, regardless the fact the homicide detectives had been sweating the block all that morning behind Bel-Bel's murder. Paula pulled onto the lot in front of the building. No one was out. She knew they played the elevators and drove around in rental cars.

Coop stood at the curb awaiting her. He walked in front. She followed him up to the lab. Paula's name was placed behind the murder and written throughout the PJ's in secret handwriting. She had no idea niggas were so cruddy and here now wanting to know who was this bitch that had appeared out of nowhere and was having motherfuckers bodied and dope fiends getting major Paypa around I4?

The first to inquire was Rook, an old school supplier for the south side projects. Bel-Bel's death was a hindrance in Rook's work being sold. Rook no longer lived in the projects, but the Paypa savage veteran still claimed to be the real estate holder of the high rise building.

He was eating off his old day's untarnished reputation. Rook was worth close to 196 stacks of small face bills of old money he had stashed after he came home from doing a ten year fed bit in Big Sandy.

It's been said, when you got gwap, you gain frienemies (friends who act like enemies).

The joint had fucked Rook's mind up! He trusted only the hand that fed him, his own! Niggas didn't want it with Rook. He had the power of the Jamaicans behind him. The whispers turned every corner about the bitch that now held the P.J.'s in a headlock with that monstrous coke.

Rook's eyes rolled over the clear sky as he stepped from his black 2003 Bentley. He always looked more valuable than he was worth. The custom whip had chrome Ashanti rims and loud beats. He crossed his arms and regarded the traffic of Paula's building for a second. It was nonstop. Funny, he no longer recalled this building making so much noise before.

Boolue, a stone cold killer who watched dogged over Rook's extravagant lifestyle, exited the passenger seat. Bel-Bel's uncle, Hampton El, exited from behind the wheel. Rook looked like a million bucks in his expensive Young American jeans, a long sleeved matching button down and crystal white sneakers.

Boolue lead the way into the building, being greeted by Half Dead, them that stood inside the lobby, he had gotten irritated at the thought of how some strange bitch had 1-4 jumping right under his nose and had those nigga's not fearing him anymore.

It was just past one in the afternoon. James heard repeated knocks at the door. The soft music of Jaheim thumped the steel door. It had iron bars on the inside. Boolue nearly choked at the sight of James opening the door.

He couldn't quite believe his eyes. Here was his old get high potna dressed like he'd been picked out to appear on Love & Hip-Hop or debut on the Tonight Show. James wore an expensive rose gold Big Meech chain and a blinding gold and diamond pinky ring. James showed off his Vernier set smile by picking his teeth with is manicured fingernails.

"This nigga stuntin!" Boolue's thoughts rambled. The two men, Boolue and James had a bit of close history that was kept quiet. At one point in Hustle City's history, they ate from the same plate and were stick-man buddies. There was no blood between them as they remembered. They'd just adventured different life paths until now. Boolue was winged by Rook as his hit man.

James was said to be strung out on that dog food so bad, that he looked like he had HIV and that he had lost his damn sanity running around robbing banks and small pocket niggas in the game. That was the sole reason Boolue was so flabbergasted to see James looking like he was getting some serious Paypa.

"What it do stranger?"

"I was just wondering how long it would be before your face made it this way!" James smiled following a moment of silence. Then he stepped aside inviting the men in which was forbidden for anyone other than family, said Paula. In this case, Uncle James went rouge.

Paula listened from the bedroom door, pissed. Rook exchanged a glance toward Boolue and Hampton El both who nodded before turning their gaze at the two heavily armed men. Wayne and Anthony Coop stood in the living room holding assault rifles. Little did Rook know, Paula had a shooter posted on the lot hiding in the trunk of a brilliant blue box Chevy. He waited for any bullshit to pop off.

"You know why I'm here, I believe," Rook asked, trying to present intimidation.

"I hope not to try threatening me," James assured.

"Na'll but you do understand this is my building," Rook added.

"Hold on, ma dude. Let's refresh yo' memory here! First of all, this the government's shit! and furthermore, I've been kicking ass up and down these hallways for over 32 years, you dig?" James nodded and faced Boolue, "So you telling me out of ten years you been knowing me, Boo, you mean you'll bounce up in ma spot with these clowns at cho hip and try an check me for this square ass nigga you barely know? I just want to hear it out of your mouth. So this is where yo heart at, huh?" James asked Boolue.

Boo frowned mildly, casting his head no. Rook peeped his response and cut into Boolue.

"Am I fuckin' talkin' to you, asshole?"

Boolue stared away followed by a nod 'no.'

"That's a cold game, Yan Ming!" Coop mumbled. He meant that towards Boolue biting his tongue for the glory of Rook's money. It was a street form of selling one's soul.

"I guess it is what it is!" said James pitting his old friend. At this point, James disregarded Boo's presence.

"Who is this chick?" Rook asked.

"Ma fuckin' niece, nigga. Why?" James popped slick.

Rook glanced at Wayne who was staring at him in combat mode.

"We gone have to figure something out and fast, cause this bitch is cutting into ma Paypa!" said Rook as he stepped closer to James.

Boolue grilled James and rolled his eyes as he followed his boss, Rook, out of the apartment slowly.

James checked the stairway for shooters after they left. He wasn't taking any chances. Lil' Dead-Head and a few others were placed on post with street sweepers. He then called Paula's name.

She stepped haughtily from behind the curtained door, her head high, chewing her gum fast. "I take it that you and that Boolue guy were friends once?" Paula noted in sarcasm.

"Still is, as a matter of fact," James answered.

Paula sat at the table placing her elbows on it with her hands folded under her chin as her mind wondered into a demonical dimension. Her eyes turned hazel when she got so upset. A light clicked on in her head. She slipped the leather strap of her Material Girl purse over her head, centering between her perfect C-cup breasts.

"I got it!" Everyone looked at her, "James, can you get me alone with Boolue, like maybe tonight?" she added biting her thumbnail.

Before James could answer, she blurted, "let's go, Coop! I'm going to take a nap. When you have him here, call me."

James' mind was in twilight. He had no clue of where this lil' girl was taking this situation, but Boolue was a real killer, Still, he nodded ok.

Later that night, the moon was full and hovering over Hustle City's meretricious, grimy, Peabody Projects.

Approximately 9:05pm that evening, Coop parked Paula's rented platinum Range Rover in the lane next to James' old school and killed his headlights. The meeting was set to take place on Fox Street in a vacant lot of the newly built town homes that sat diagonally from Peabody's preschool. Paula exited the truck in a bright red Freakum dress skirt and six inch black red bottom peek toe stilettos. Her face was covered in BeBe's foundation and wet lip gloss. She walked to the back of the passenger door of the Lexus and gestured for Coop to open the door for her. He did as he was directed. She climbed in as if no problem. "So, you're that parasite's winning lottery ticket, huh?" Paula asked.

Boolue lubricated his lips. "You could say that. Big balls, ok! I like that in you," he stated.

Paula gazed into his whip. It was the older model Lexus. Boolue laughed pretty boy massaging his goatee.

"Ok, let's get straight to business!" she continued. "This is where yo' life changes and you could get rid of this old ass bitch car and hop into something foreign. It's simple. I want you to body Rook, like tonight!

Then meet me at 1-4," she added.

Boolue froze his smile. "What the fuck! Is you insane, woman?" he cursed.

Quick on her feet, Paula responded, "no, insanity is allowing yourself to go through life being beat down when you have a lion locked inside of you and you're the only one with the key to unleash that beast which holds you prisoner toward the very reality you reject as insanity." As Paula closed her spill, she leaned closer to him. "He mistreats you and disrespects you.

I'm better. I can give you the run of his whole operation. I'll supply you with enough coke to run these projects with my uncles. Think about it.

It's simple. Like I said, either you wanna get rich with us or go to war for the reptile that only uses you."

Paula was right and he knew it. Boolue stared at the diva in lust and respect. Her body was tense. She would never trust him. "Shit, your balls are bigger than I thought," said Boolue.

What Paula had said had made a lot of sense to him. She re-glossed her lips. Coop stood outside Boolue's side window. It was half opened. He pointed his burning cigarette at Paula. "If he don't you know I'll body that lil' disrespectful son of a bitch!" said Coop.

Paula ended the debate when she showered the bundle of big faces into Boo's lap. "Here, that's ten stacks as a down payment. Do the job and I'll hit chu with another 40 when I see it on the ten o'clock news." Paula had signed her first paid hit.

Boolue handed the money back. "I like the first agreement. I wanna eat from yo' plate. I'm feeling the way you treat yo' soldiers," he said sliding the money back into her lap.

"No, you mean family sweetheart. We family," Paula corrected him.

"Consider him dead," was Boolue's last words.

"You one bad bitch!" said Coop as they pulled away beating Plies *Worth Goin' Fed Fo'*!

CHAPTER THIRTEEN - Judas

The President of the United States aired his State of the Union address on CNN News.

President Barack Obama has connoted and doomed Congressman Blake Griffen to hereby disenchant the 25 year Human Rights Bill. That African Americans shouldn't have to be *reconsidered* to vote as an American citizen. He further explained, the unsightly and often bizarre functioning of a government lacking social graces and tranquility as promised by a genocidal drug (crack cocaine) targeted towards African Americans, Latinos and poor white trash, causing them to serve harsher penalties than those who manufacture powder cocaine. Obama signed into law the 18 to 1 retroactive crack bill.

Diamond and Paula took note of the good news heading out on a three hour G6 flight that evening to gather Mother's Day gifts. Mainly for Paula, an alibi while Boolue took care of Rook back in St. Louis.

The following morning, the girls watched Obama's live broadcast from a 30 inch monitor at the east coast famous, 25 Park Boutique. They paired with sleek black pants and lace up boots by Marc Jacobs that complimented their long sleeved pastel pink lace blouses. Diamond carried Tiger like he was a baby.

At nearly 1,000 miles away, back in Hustle City, at approximately 12:40, dressed in Zyion denim jeans and purple Black Label sweater and a pair of Black Label boots and a princess cut yellow stone Paul-Wall watch hugging his right wrist.

Rook sat behind the wheel of his candy purple rain drop colored Jaguar on black dub Davins. His music softly thumped. He was on his way to discuss his options with his cousin, Jamaican Claud. He considered switching from cocaine to heroin.

The numbers were like night and day. Simple, you making close to 36 thousand a kilo in the projects were going to be a thing of the past for him after today, so he planned. Unfortunately, he had received an emergency call from Boolue before he had the chance to tell his guys the good news.

"I got this bad ass bitch waiting beside me! She trying 'na get at chu, fool!" Boolue lied.

"Shid, send me a picture of da ho!" Rook requested.

"Fool, it should be hitting you as we speak!" The photo covered Rook's cell screen. The picture was one of Diamond that Paula had taken of her one day stepping out of the shower wrapped in a beige-colored beach towel. They'd been playing around. Diamond's hair was wet, which made her look like something from an island. Paula had snapped a full boob shot.

Rook was a freak for red bones. Claud would have to meet him later. He planned to have ole girl with him when they did. The cousins loved stuntin!

Rook was on his merry way to meet Baby. He felt a wave of lust between his legs. Finally, he arrived. Boolue wasn't where he said he'd be. He waited on the lot for nearly three minutes. Rook never waited on people. People waited on his mental clock, as he put it. In this case he wanted to gut ol' girl badly. He dialed Boo's cell. No answer.

Suddenly, he saw his man step from between two parked SUV's. Boolue climbed into the Jag, not exactly closing his door behind him. Rook stared at him wondering, 'where in the fuck was Baby?' "Nigga, yo' ass know I don't do no waiting on no motherfuckers! Real talk! And where is baby girl?" he grilled.

"She finna bounce out that crib right there," Boolue pointed across Rook's chest. He lied, gripping the forty in his right pocket.

Rook's cell vibrated as he looked away. It was Jamaican Claud waiting impatiently at Mamma Jammer's Soul Foods on Natural Bridge and King's Highway. He had his girl Ziggy with him, who kept him on point about laundering his money. Rook glanced down at the face of the incoming call. Boolue's eyes nervously rotated the area for nosy witnesses. No one was there but two junky whores working the track on Chaudoe Street.

It was now or never. His finger closed over the trigger as Rook held the Apple phone smashed to his face. Boolue raised the forty in the direction and pulled the trigger twice.

The blast was deafening in the small car. The flame lit the interior. Rook's brains scattered over his dash and driver's window as the bullet deflected out the top of the whip. The human flesh popped into Boo's face. The blow-back was nauseating for him, but, it was the price you sometimes paid when you done a 187 at point blank range.

The kid had sold his loyalty just as Judas had crossed Jesus. He leaned back against the door and furthered his assault on Rook's slumped body. There was no need for him to check Rook's pulse. The kid was long gone.

He calmly exited the vehicle, then fled between the buildings. Rook had never even noticed that Boolue entered the car wearing brownie gloves.

Boolue called James from the Broadway White Castle he had trotted to. James answered immediately.

"ma dude, we good!" Boolue whispered unclothing himself in the restroom, exhausted from the top speed sprint. James hurried to him with a change of clothes then retrieved Rook's cell from Boolue.

He was smart. He destroyed the tiny simm card that held Diamond's photo as bad as he wanted to keep them.

Later that night, Paula, Linda and Diamond landed at the Lambert's Airport with tons of labeled shopping bags. The girls had a blast like they always have when they were together. It was like Carmello, Kobe and LeBron playing for Phil Jackson.

Coop and Paula drove to his older brother's spot on Ann, off South Jefferson, where they waited for Boolue and Uncle James' arrival. Not long afterwards they entered through the back door. Paula was tired and cranky with jet lag. She wasted no time. She dug in her bra and tossed Boolue a stack of hundreds.

"Welcome to the family. I like ma people fresh and loyal." She stared at him knowing that he'd just crossed his own man. She'll never let that escape her subconscious. He would sell her out as well, if given a better deal from some competition. Paula stepped to the window that viewed a beautiful night sky covered in stars as the St.

Louis police department sirens ran crazy throughout Hustle City. Everybody and their momma was back in the coke business due to Obama passing the 18 to 1 crack bill. Crime has picked up, Paula thought, as she stood there in silence a few stories up from the busy streets below her. She was about to be three times above the game.

CHAPTER FOURTEEN – Party Girls

Paula felt as light as a feather and untouchable. This was all going to work out. Everything had been falling in her favor. Uncle James and Boolue had locked the projects down. The money began rolling in ten-fold hence.

1-4 attracted more ladies that moved in only to be under the 1-4 Mob. They were balling out of control!

Crum Snatching Anna, as she was called, and her daughter Kim had moved next door to James' spot. He ended up smashing Anna on the reg. Paula had seen her suppliers three times that month.

It was a bright cool day. The queen, Paula, felt like a walk. She had never actually walked around the P.J.'s. She was always in and out. Today, she wanted to stretch her legs and let the lil' young popcorn hoes first hand know who the baddest bitch was around Hustle City. She was getting the big head. Coop walked beside her watching their surroundings. Paula wore a Sex Code spandex body suit with a black waist high ruffled leather jacket and a pair of six inch Sex Code Caliente black quarter length summer leather boots. Hoes had to stand down.

Paula's hair was whipped in a feather style with Burgundy bangs. Sweet Shears was her chosen salon. She strolled down the west side of 14th Street. She occasionally glanced at the parking lot full of doe boys being shook down by the jump out boys, special force police unit.

"That's my work!" she said in such a smile.

This was her first look at Tearence. He leaned against a candy painted Dodge Avenger sitting on chrome foe's. His swag was different from the average project dude. He carried that deep country look. He had the nuts to assure her that there were no questions, he was at that. The kid who knew who she was, and Coop wasn't all that friendly looking.

"The hell with it. The whole fucking city knew who she was and who else better to have her than me?" Tearence mumbled to his boy, Hozay.

"Nigga, you gone get our damn heads knocked off, fuckin' with that crazy ass bitch!" said Hozay.

"Lady Face, huh," he mumbled.

That's what everybody called Paula around the P.J.'s.

"You think you fancy, huh?" he yelled.

She ignored him and admired that he had the balls to buck Coop and say something to her.

"So you gone play it like that, Shawty? Let a real nigga step with chu!" the voice added.

Coop looked at her for her consent to cut into ole' boy.

She gave no such. Paula loved a good challenge. She glanced at him with an intriguing, inviting smile. She was going to bone him! It was already decided. He was definitely swagged out. Hot and cocky, just how she was used to 'em. It was just something about them thug niggaz that made her wet and want more of them. The next time Paula saw Tearence was two months later. It was her born day, May 27, the same as Coop's sister Toby's B-day, as well. The girls planned to have a dual sweet 30th bash at the Lamear Casino. Paula wasn't sparing any financial burials the day of their births. It was all out ball out. She arranged for Coop's mother, Chi-Chi, to make all the necessary arrangements. Chi-Chi was said to have done some great bashes for even celebs such as Mick Jagger and Miley Cyrus.

All she had been told was that the girls wanted to party like rock stars and to get wasted.

Chi-Chi did what she do. She hired caterers from Miami and have the event broadcast on local satellite radio. Doors were set to open at 6 P.M. and ladies were always free until 1 A.M.

Chi-Chi booked Lupe Fiasco, Avante, and Rick Ross. Just Bleezy and the All-Stars were set as the opening act, but were replaced due to the famous star Just Bleezy himself was indicted for five kilograms of powder coke.

To Chi-Chi "Without a clear vision, success is impossible!"

The city was going to celebrate Paula's born day as if it was theirs. The theme of the bash was 'Diva Fresh'. It was air brushed on her invitations and concert tickets. It was like a swap meet. Plenty of heavyweights attended at their best. The signup sheet was full. The line continued to grow with out-of-towners. Paula pulled up on notice in the Vale Lane followed by Diamond, who rode shotgun with Toby in her new black Q-5 truck that Paula bought her sista-in-law.

Paula's Lambo doors winged open on the banana Testerosa. Her yellow 6 inch Gucci Stilettos hit the pavement. Photographers circled her car, camera flashes dazzled from her big face Gucci shades. They mistook her for Toya Carter. Escorted by Coop, she stood momentarily outside the exotic sports car, then headed towards the entrance. She wore a beautiful yellow silk evening gown made by Gucci Lurfer that set off her blond micro braids. She wore some serious diamond studs in her ears and a seven thousand dollar Lady's Cartier wrist watch. Around her ankle, she wore a diamond tennis bracelet that matched the diamond platinum around her neck. It had her beloved sister's name CARLA engraved on it in palace script.

The girls grinned as they walked past the party goers waiting to enter her bash. Now she knew what Linda and Diamond felt being widow rich and sizzling single. Diamond looked stunning in her Freak Um Sex Code curvy gown and matching open toe micro tip 6 inch stilettos. Tony and Evelyn were at their best rocking tight ass Kim & Khole low-rise Dash jeans and heel boots. Linda was the head turner though. She had gotten her hair cut in a Halle Berry style. She too, wore pants that were fitted. They were white leather Apple Bottoms. She rocked body paints as a top covering. She had a breast augmentation done as a surprise to her girls.

She was like Evelyn on *Basketball Wives*. She hated to be outdone, although she loved Paula. It was a girl thing. Paula's girls were on point.

"Beautiful ladies please be seated," said the host, Trey Songz, waving them to their VIP seats. Tables filled with bottles and balloons, and male strippers began to appear around their tables and on stage.

Paula's eyes popped and the men went straight at her. The replacement of Just Bleezy, Tankee Luciano and Mardigrameech came to the stage relpin say no mo entertainment without delay. The music shook the casino as the night dwindled with fun.

Paula flagged her assigned waiter, Tank, who quickly appeared at her feet. She was wasted and past the point of wanting to sit on a dick.

"Three bottles of Freaky-Moscato please," she ordered, rubbing his naked chest in drunken lust.

He vanished. When he returned, he popped their corks and refilled their glasses. The divas all clinked their glasses in a toast to Carla and Paula's mother, Pam. The moment and booze tore into Paula, she was a softie when it came to her mother and her lil' sister, Carla. Her face crumbled into tears.

"Let's party!" Toby screamed to veer her mind back on getting wasted.

It worked and they did so. Paula got on stage with Nelly and the Lunatics and bounced her luscious ass followed by the pretty girl rock as if she invented the dance.

Ass was everywhere. Niggas were blowing that paper like they printed that shit. When Paula left the stage, Coop was there following her every move.

He never let her out of his sight. He had taken her jewelry for safekeeping.

Paula sat in VIP ate spicy party wings and sipped her drinks. She noticed Tearence sitting at the nearby bar alone. She watched him over the rim of her drinks.

"Are you following me?" she asked with a smile as he stepped to her.

"If that's what you say it is," he added, holding his Spade bottle to his chest.

Linda and Diamond sat alone chatting over their plans to deal with the situation at work.

The tsunami was devastating in Japan. F.E.M.A. declared emergency medical help for 1/4 of the victims. They were set to be arriving at the hospital late the following day.

Paula and Tearence enjoyed their moment.

"So you ready to start fucking with a real nigga, or what?" he asked.

She glanced over the print between his legs. She was horny. They chatted through a few more songs then exchanged numbers. He saved hers into his black Droid and kissed her cheek softly as she stood up.

Coop hated it!

"Holla at me ma," he added, smiling toward Coop.

She watched the impressionable guy of her dreams walk back to his bros who gave him hugs and daps. They knew their boy had scored big once again. It was a pleasure for his man Hozay to see. Being that he thought he was the one who taught him what he knows.

Tearence and Hozay were tied tight. They copped a quarter kilo of cocaine together. They were chemist when it came to dry cooking cocaine. It was their reason of stuntin' so hard.

Later that night, he called her.

She gladly invited him over. She was drunk out of her mind by the time he arrived at her home. She opened the door. He stepped in.

"Damn you smell good," he lusted,

Paula was turned on by the sound of his voice. She led him to the second level. She had recently moved from Diamond's into a baby mansion across the street from Tommy Tucker. She switched on the lights from her master panel in the foyer. He followed her into the bedroom. Paula opened her pink see through teddy revealing her amazing naked body. He had a hard on with plenty to start on.

"Happy birthday to me!"

Condoms lay at his reach in a jewelry box on her night stand. After she teased him to a near pre-cum, she gave it to him.

Their moans and groping played like music until the sun rose. Paula awoke with a massive headache. The bright sun was shining through the windows. Tearence got up and heard the shower water running. Paula appeared wearing his button down shirt. She looked even more sexier with wet hair draped over her shoulders. He held the image in his mind.

"Did you enjoy yo' b-day?" he asked, groping himself over the pink silk sheet.

"I don't know. It's not over yet!" she returned, climbing on top of him.

He felt like it was his birthday as well. She was surely a treat. She placed her palms under his shoulders and laced her thin fingers over them. He relaxed onto his back as the birthday girl pleasurably dug her knees and toe tips into the therapeutic mattress. The arch in her back flexed.

Tearence was being hit by her as if he were a hoe with her legs bound behind her head. He didn't have to work hard to satisfy her hunger, judging Paula's moans. He was packing hard or soft. His sex was a thick meaty, nine inches and seemed everlasting to her. He grinded at her grooves with slow, deep strokes into her wetness. He could feel Paula was near her third climax.

He pulled out of her each time her vagina muscles would flex and reflex.

He wanted her to burn alive for more of him.

She thirsted in words, "Baby, please stay deep!" she moaned while holding the back of his thighs to prevent him from pulling out. Without physical tears, she cried inside. She had never had a man that knew all of her sex tricks and had the skills to control his climax at the same time.

He had the real magic stick, she thought.

His lesbian sister had taught him all the secrets to pleasing women. At any moment, if he'd only asked, Paula would have let him in on her big secret of her being broken in young and now as an adult, enjoyed anal.

During the following weeks after Paula's birthday, Tearence and her became inseparable.

"Why don't you let me and the guys sell 'dat shit for you?" Tearence asked.

"Cause I don't want our personal relationship to interfere with my business. And trust me, I'm a whole 'nother person when it comes to my paper," Paula added, turning her eyes up and down at him. "And I must say, I like us how we are, so let's keep that in the bag, ok sweetie?"

"Look here baby girl, I'm not asking you for no handouts. You ain't gotta front us shit. We got our own paper!" he assured her, obviously offended.

Either way, it didn't matter to Paula. She had all the winning cards in her pocket. Life was a game of chess to her and she was good at it. She gassed him seriously.

"So tell me, how much change do you have of your own? Tell momma," she asked, kissing him.

He gripped the cuff of her ass-cheeks. "Well, we got," he started to say.

"No, no, no! I asked how much you as a whole have. Not yo' lil' friends!"

He looked into her eyes, dumbfounded.

Paula wanted him to start counting his own paper if he was going to claim her; he had to upgrade his swag. Meaning his friends would immediately become his lil' guys. Paula had basically asked him to go from zero to sixty within a matter of a centimeter of a second. Her offer made no sense to him. He agreed anyway. It was a win-win situation.

Paula placed her index finger over his words. "Shh, Momma got cha," she added softly.

"I know damn well this broad ain't just tried to lil' boy me!" Tearence murmured as he watched Paula walk naked out of the room with a sassy look over her shoulder.

She knew that she had just handled his ass. She returned within a couple of minutes. She then tossed a tan wrapped package into his naked lap as she simultaneously flopped back onto her bed. "I guess you got your piece of cake on my b-day and ate it too, huh? Just make sure the next meeting we have, you have my 20 gs with you. And baby boy, don't make me have to come looking for you over two punk ass dimes."

Tearence sat the 1008 grams of Lady Gaga on the night stand and put his arms around her. Surely, Paula was the boss in the streets, but Tearence ruled her bedroom and Paula bowed to him each time he laid that nine inch muscle on her ass. Finally, she'd met her match in the sex game.

Tearence stuck to his word and delivered the 20 thousand to Paula later that evening. He fronted most of the drugs to his man Gino Grap after he first stepped on the coke. It came back to exactly 54 ounces as she said. Tearence shook his package as he said within 3 days. Cook Avenue was dry of cocaine. Tearence pulled in $51,800 at $700 an ounce. He contacted his tenda with the cash. Paula was pleased. She met him at Gold's Gym. He handed Coop the gym bag.

"I see you've been busy," said Paula.

Coop stood there with the bag drawn over his shoulder. He watched Tearence closely. Uncle James told Coop that he never trusted that lil' mothafucka for as far as he could see him. He warned Coop to be prepared to shoot him at any time. James was almost sure Tearence may try to rob his niece. Paula told her beau to meet her at the McDonald's on Lindell at 9:15 A.M.

Time seemed to fast forward for Tearence. 9:15 A.M. was only minutes away on his watch. It was the perfect day for him to put miles on his 1150 Hyabusa street bike. It was Paula's favorite color, canary yellow with chrome Labron rims.

He rode fast. There was no doubt whatever Paula wanted was very important.

The motorcycle's engine rumbled in the parking lot exactly on time. He parked beside her virgin white Benz 500. He climbed into the passenger's seat.

He looked at Coop seated in Paula's rear seat.

The men's vibes were bland. Coop never spoke. Ever.

"Here," she handed him three bricks.

He looked surprised. "What's this?" he asked.

"Since you gone be my baby's father, I figured I'd help you get on your feet before the baby is born. Cause you won't be in these streets if I can help it." She smiled. "I'm pregnant."

"Damn, are you serious?"

Coop scuffled around in the back seat. It was the last thing he'd wanted to tell James.

"Aw, fuck!" Tearence moaned, slumping into his seat. He knew he was in Paula's purse forever at this point of the game. Finally, his dick game had paid off. "Damn man!" He knew at this point, there was a high chance of him losing his boys forever between Paula's controlling ways. And them not running up in Strip Clubs as they use too.

"What chu mean by *damn*? So, you don't want my baby?" she gritted.

"N'all crazy ass woman! It's not that. I'm just excited," he lied.

She smiled.

He kissed her excitingly. "It's all good beau. I gotta go," he glanced at his watch feeling like Tommy Red when he had Maywest. Tearence tied the package Paula had given him under the black net strapped to the tail of his bike. He discreetly pulled away.

Paula watched him through her rearview. She had to test his loyalty before she birthed his child. She aligned her gaze into the light tinted windows of the McDonald's. She focused on the man who stood at the cash register.

She entered the establishment calmly. The man there looked up from the register. He inhaled her Britney Spears Radiance perfume in lust.

"May I help you, beautiful?" he smiled.

"This mother fucker doesn't even know who I am," she thought. It enraged Paula. "Oh, since I ain't eating out of yo' trash can, you don't know me no more, huh!?" she hissed.

Carlos narrowed his eyes to place her. She was the recollection lit in his eyes. His face turned from curious to flabbergasted. He licked his lips as he admired her grown and sexy.

"Back for more, huh?" he laughed.

"Yeah, an I'll be right back!" she left and returned two minutes later with Coop. Paula ordered his new combo with a banana split while Coop identified Carlos. The minute Carlos handed her the hot meal, he said, "You like it hot now, huh?" He said teasing her about eating the cold food from the garbage.

He laughed. She snatched it then stormed out the glass door.

Carlos leaned out the drive-thru window and saw Paula's spotless Mercedes neon blue lights pop on. "Damn, that bitch lookin good now and I know it's still good!" he lustfully grunted.

"Man you know damn well yo' uncircumcised dick ain't hit that, ever!" one of his co-workers was sure of that.

Carlos began bragging about how they were fucking on the regular. He lied on his dick.

Paula parked around the corner and waited. She had called Tearence back to the restaurant. It was an emergency. His hood, Cook Avenue, being only minutes away from the Mickey D's on Lindell and Sarah. He pulled up in a snap and parked behind Paula. She told him the Carlos situation. Of course, she left out the part about her eating trash and being a junkie.

Tearence and Coop seated his bike.

"What he look like?" Tearence asked.

"Coop knows. He'll finger him for you," she added.

The two men made their way back to the McDonald's. They entered the establishment at 9:56 P.M., just before Carlos' break. Tearence glanced over to Coop who sat at a table eating a Big Mac. He nodded toward Carlos behind the counter. Tearence bucked the black plastic Glock and walked up to him.

"A hommie, let me holla at chu!" he hissed.

Carlos turned to face the voice.

Tearence looked over to Coop to confirm once again this was his target.

Coop again nodded yes. Tearence pulled the Glock from behind him and pointed it in Carlos' face. He squeezed the trigger.

The flame flashed bright. The bullet exploded Carlos' left brow. Customers hit the deck and trampled out of both doors! A huge mist of blood covered the air before Carlos' body slammed between the fryers. Tearence aimed and fired several more rounds into him to be sure.

Each bullet found their target. The men fled the scene.

The victim was rushed to the hospital. He was survived by his wife and two children. The panicking staff had described the suspect as a tall black male, standing about 6 feet with a medium build, wearing a white shirt with blue and gold sleeves, blue jeans and a red STL baseball cap and dark sunglasses.

I guess it's true. You really don't see shit when them cannons bustin'.

The police had no suspects on the case. This was only the beginning of the few scores Paula had to settle before she birthed her baby. It had taken the diva weeks to get over the enthusiasm of having her first child. Her B.D. Tearence was taking off in the dope game. He was bigger than ever before.

The pot-naz he once thought he had, envied his advance as Paula said they would. They didn't understand his bitch breaking him off with the cheapest weight in the city and that they couldn't deal first hand with her being they were his boys and would blindly go to war beside him like Leonardo and the 300 Spartans. Tearence's paper was made in the barrels of Hustle City's Central West End area on Cook Avenue, which became Paula's new headquarters.

Bonded through the unborn child she carried of Cook's bread winner, Tearence, whose crazy ass cousin Palo had just come home from Terre Haute USP Fed joint for bodying some fool on some disrespect towards his Eight Tray Hoova gang.

CHAPTER FIFTEEN – Mo' Money – Mo' Problems

Paula's next score presented through the following two months. Her diva was beyond what niggaz could ever imagine. Her inner self-worth continued to thrive through it all. As a homeless, addicted whore, who after losing her all, continued on despite the loss of her sister and mother.

Just as they say, "the mo' money, the mo' problems!" Her vindictive ambition grew unpredictable by the second month of her pregnancy with Tearence's baby girl. Paula thought she would have twins. It felt like she was carrying two souls inside of her, whose name would soon be Jenna. Paula wanted a clean slate for Jenna. To meet those expectations she had to handle Peter's dog ass first handed before the few others she wanted erased. She had long considered retiring after what she thought of as bringing her lil' sister's spirit back through her baby's birth. Peter was a mission only she could tackle alone, if she expected any true closure within. Her hands and feet turned cold at the thought of him. Having Uncle James or Coop handle it wouldn't be near as satisfying as seeing his blood being spilled by her hands.

Paula rose from her bedroom at Diamond's condo that she often used as a sanctuary for peace when her brain overloaded or when she was irate at Tearence's flirtatious ass! She shaved her revealing body hairs. She whipped her silky hair into a rap style and covered it with a vogue wig and clothed herself in a Yves Saint Laurant hoodie sweat suit that hugged between her camel toe.

She slipped on her Y.V.S.L. leather gloves. The hoodie was placed over her blonde streaked wig. She popped in a pair of lake green contacts and left Diamond a note posted on their 'things to do' list.

Love always, Paula, she signed, then stormed out of the house and proceeded to calmly ease her way down two blocks out of her nosey neighbor's sight until she reached a vacant house which she used as a cut that led her through a few back yards to a raindrop colored menace to society 5.0 that she copped from an anonymous crack fiend, something she referred to as 'a geek swerve'.

She was nervous, but business had to be handled. She could see them vividly as if they were her own hands touching the victims. She aimed to use a woman's most trusted tool. The way her mother gutted Carla's murderers roamed nonstop through her pretty skull. This would be the 'perfect storm,' she timely thought.

Tiny droplets of rain dotted her windshield as she raced through the high winds and cloudy skies heading across Grand Boulevard, towards what she thought of as the *Dead Zone*, while listening to Nikki Minaj's *I Am Monster*.

Within thirty minutes she caught up with ole' dog ass Peter riding down Martin Luther King Drive checking his usual trap spots near the Wellston Loop.

"Peter!" Paula shouted as she sped beside him, honking her horn.

Peter smelled of three day worn clothes covered in Usher cologne. She smashed her Khole Dash shades onto her face. Peter adjusted his rearview. He noticed Paula's pink lip gloss.

"Yes sir, I got da ass!"

He was curious of the driver as he pulled onto the BP's lot on Union and Martin Luther King. His chrome foe's kept spinning. Paula pulled up fast to his driver's door hooded up.

"Peter, what's up baby?" she noted.

He reached at his heat revealed from his waist.

"This Paula! Let me holla at chu big head!" she yelled.

"Goddamn girl, don't do that shit out here! I damn near shot that bitch up!"

Paula chuckled only to fog his focus and suspicions.

"This nut looks like he's been smoking that glass dick," she seriously thought noticing the heavy dark rings around his eyes. He had to be holess she thought, his spot had been pumping so hard and as everyone knew, he was that fuckin' greedy that he'd began working his packs solo-doe-lo! She agreed to follow him a few blocks over to his cousin Big Ray Ray Sykes' condo to park his whip.

Paula did as he requested. DMX's *What Chu Want* whispered in his ears as he entered her 5.0.

He smiled and assured himself of just what Paula wanted. He unzipped his True Religion jeans and manhandled his mild limp dick over his lap in her gaze as she pulled from behind his whip.

"Where you going girl? You could jump on this mother fucka right now. I ain't got time for this romantic shit!" he warned her jacking at his meat.

Paula, like all ladies, couldn't miss a peek at that dick. She glanced at it unintentionally. She then added volume to the Alpine versing Eminem & Rihanna *Love the Way You Lie*.

"That'll be the last hard on yo' ugly ass'a ever get!" she mumbled driving fast down Page.

Peter stared at her silence, hesitatingly. "What chu thinking about so quiet? And where in the hell are you taking me to? Yo' ass know it's check day out here. I'm on ma grind right now," he said pulling off her hoodie which fell onto her shoulders.

Her face loosened. She spoke, "Man, don't worry. When I get done, you won't be thinking about any money. Um'ma give you everything you should've gotten long ago." She smiled.

Peter manly tugged at his crotch, reading it for the believed anal sex Paula had for him; although she had nothing else he hadn't taken from her already. Her world was once again his, he felt, each time he stood on her neck.

"You know, I've been missing this shit for a long time now and you dun got back thick!" he lusted. "You know um' ma punish it, don't chu?" he noted, leaning toward her planting an alcohol tasting kiss at the crack of her wet lips. He continued, "You know something baby, on some real talk. Deep in yo heart you know you always had the keys to my heart," he lied. "Baby I know we have been through a lot coming up in this concrete jungle out here without a solid education, or any family that really give a fuck enough to steer us in the right direction." His eyes teared. "Paula, I wish we could just leave this place and escape through open trees finding ourselves walking down another yellow brick road heading back to that small place called Kansas like Diana Ross when she played Dorothy in the Wizard of Oz," he heartfully testified laughing on the inside knowing Paula always fell victim to his gift of gab spills. He was high on oxy.

"Oh really!" she snarled, flipping him off.

"Baby, on ma' momma, I know what I've done to us in the past was dead wrong, fucked up out there. I've leveled all that shit out since. You don't know, but I've been going to church trying to get ma shit straight. I swear baby,

I was gone come find you!" he lied.

"Peter, please. Don't do that shit. You don't have to sit here and curse God when I already know better, boy. So please stop trying to use that stale ass game on me. It's so like yesterday. I'm a grown-ass Mrs. now. Plus, I'm already pregnant by a decent dude that respects me like a lady and..."

"Bitch! Respect you?" He cut Paula's sentence short. "I got cho respect right here, ho!" Peter's huge palm cracked across her now rose coloring red cheek. Paula's 5.0 zig-zagged the road. She whined like old brakes.

"Now hurry up and stop this mother fuckin' car and buckle down on this dick, dope head hoe and handle yo' business cum freak slut, sittin' here faking like you cut like that, playing games with me!" he cursed, choking Paula at the back of her neck.

Paula responded quickly in both fear and revenge. That was the straw breaker she needed. And to think she almost spared his stanky ass! Believing he found God listening to all that noise he was talking. She savagely pulled into Stevence School yard bobbing her head in a yes motion. Her palms gripped tightly at the sweaty steering wheel until her arms grew heavy. Her small painted toes inside of her number four Jay's eased from the accelerator with weak knees sliding to a sudden halt at the vacant school's rear gated playground near an infamous hood diva's house named Lil' Tina.

"You got that shit right. The game have raped us both young and you very much has taken everything from me and that's something I'll never get back," Paula argued, fingering through her Y.V.S.L. purse as Peter mustered his jeans to his ankles for her to do what she always had during his mad spells.

A streak of sun frowned through the crack of the dark rain clouds at center top of the hard top 5.0.

Paula cried out as she plunged a twelve inch blade toward him, the same as the one ole' girl used in the movie Carrie. She quickly pounded into Peter's balled chest viciously.

"I hate you! *Bastard!*" she cried out.

He felt her many years of pain through the point of her knife penetrating his evil flesh making love to the leather seat he slumped in. Paula was possessed with the Omen of Death. It felt good. Peter's blood melted into the interior as he threw blows to her face. She felt nothing. The tender force of her left hand clawed its way into Peter's thin throat holding him at bay. Paula stared into his pitiful eyes as if he were an infectious disease touching her skin.

She screamed, "Mono-Y-Mono mother fucker," as Carla's loving voice scrambled through her forbidden evil mind.

"Paula, stop! It's over. I see him. He's gone the other way." Carla's voice spoke of him going to hell. Peter slumped there lifeless with seventeen punctures in him. Paula slammed her back onto the blood stained windshield and dashboard exhaustedly straddling his nakedness. Her nipples grew.

Paula torched Peter's corpse along with the unmarked 5.0. after changing out of her bloody clothes and returned home by Yellow Cab Service.

She kept it 100 and stuck to the script with closed lips. She rested beside Diamond's lesbian ass, cuddled like a baby rubbing her own stomach, anxious to get back to her paper chase.

Tearence, Uncle James, Coop and Paula's entire crew called her platinum diamond smart phone. She ignored it and stayed low.

CHAPTER SIXTEEN – Perfect Place 4 a Perfect Death

Friday, June 25, Paula's vacation was over and the heat of her kill was over. Her cell, Twitter and Facebook page was clogged with unanswered calls, message and tweets.

"Oh my God!" She was more amazed at how much so many people depended on her ties to function. She replied punching the little keys on her device as her and Diamond sat at their table enjoying their breakfast. Eggs, sausage, grits and strawberry preserves on French toast.

"Yummy," Paula grunted to Carla's favorite. "The PJ's need love!" her first message read. "Lil girl, you think this is a game? You know I ain't had no ass in 3 days. Where are you and my baby? Love ya # 'yo B.D. Tearence," she read aloud with much joy on her beautiful face.

Diamond laughed with tight eyes, her fantasy of spreading her wet pussy lips over Paula's glossy lips just as she did that jelly.

Moments later, Paula's frame hurried from the table to do her diva thing before heading out to breast feed her city with coke.

Paula's life was about to change in ways she had never imagined. She headed out the door Lindsay Lohan style, stupid, rich blonde, with a *fuck the universe* swag. She had just gotten away with cold blooded murder. Her hands itched for more. "I wish a motherfucker would play games with ma paper!" She dared anyone biting her bottom lip coming to the conclusion of what her new name would now be. I'm going by *China*! She stared at herself.

Meanwhile, at this very same time, Paula's squad dealt with their own dilemma. Silence mourned on C.A. Cook Avenue. As a trilogy of platinum 745 BMW's crashed the set foolin' packed with Rook's Jamaican half cousin and main supplier, Jamaican Claud.

"Take one of mine, me all devour everything you love!" was the laws Freddy-B and his 'Rude Boy' posse lived by. For whacking Rook it waved war for the coke queen and her rehabilitated crew.

Judging the power moves Paula and her small army were capable of pulling off, her organization seemed much larger than the tight circle of 19 she held close to her breast.

'Rude Boy Claud' swore she was responsible and had fucked with some true monsters from the islands. Who could stop someone who lived by a death wish and was born with an empty soul, like a Taliban? These blood thirsty animals continued their killing spree at the very life of Paula child's father, Tearence.

Claud followed Tearence as he turned onto Cook Avenue, crossing Redd Foxx Lane. It was high noon. Cool humidity lingered from the three-day long rain. Tearence's, 2010 Denali SUV curbed at the 3700 block, Cook Apartment Complex, where hood dreams were created overnight.

The jamaicans despised the fact Cook was under siege by anyone other than the Rude Boy cartel, though they had a death grip throughout the hood during the early 90's by Freddy-B's brothers, Paul and Reco, who died middle aged by gun smoke at the hand of some jack boys. The legendary Sweet-P and Lafar.

Paula had put down some crucial blow forging her way to the top of street cred. Motherfuckers called her dope, "That's Mrs. Frank White!" The Rude Boys were pushing nearly 152 bricks of boy throughout central Missouri, manufactured from Queens' Projects.

St. Louis had never been hit this hard by heroin.

As Tearence unseated his truck with a Colt .45 lined at his waist. He headed to his third floor trap spot where he planned to meet his B-M Paula to re-up. Cook continued to move work as it had during the days Mike Meeks and Yum-Yum were shakin' the spot. Everyone held onto their last packs busting them down until Paula hit the scene. Crackheads and distant traffic mobbed the set begging for weight and better deals on the breakdown. There wasn't nothing shaking but plenty of dog food. No one sold anything over an eight ball of coke and only a limited number of grams of their dog food (heroin.) The queen had finally reached the city limits where she felt comfortable. She powered her phone with her freshly done nails. Just as the diva's beau Tearence's Apple phone vibrated through his $300 dollar Young Americas jean pocket. A dreaded flunky with orange Adidas track pants calmly unseated the rear door of the second Beemer. It was an older half Jamaican with Kongo dreads who swore on his dead mother that he'll slam that hammer in the drop of a dime for the Rude Boys for rec alone just to show his appreciation to Claud for pulling him out of the gutta of the Harlem slums. He was a junky. He had now ran up behind Tearence at the rear location of his SUV. Just as Tearence right foot touched the sidewalk, the Rude Boy placed something cold and stiff with an 8" barrel onto the base of Tearence's cranium with force! The man spoke with a generic Russian accent as he ordered his prey onto his knees. Shit had gotten bloody.

"Blood me pappa!" he shouted and fired off spirts of buckshots that dug fragments of Tearence's skull into the dusty cracks of the sidewalk without blinking once. The Rosta then waved his barrel toward the scattering crowd.

"Rude Boy! Bom 'Ba Clot!" he yelled from the window of the 745 Beemer as it's 22 inch Davens cut smoke heading toward Grand Crossing Spring firing rounds into Hustle City's cloudy skies.

The statement the bloody Jamaicans had made was shocking. Paula was contacted immediately by both her Uncle James and Anthony Coop. Her heart turned.

Her reason to escape her past laid there at the crossroads for Rook's blood she had spilled long ago.

There was no way she could believe Tee was gone so soon, but it was true.

Paula had to witness her lover's corpse with her own two eyes. She flashed through stop signs and red lights finding her way hood bound, weathered with tears covering Tearence's bloody torso. She held her lover guarded by Tearence's people until the ambulance and police arrived. He was pronounced DOA. The police loved to see young black men fall at the hands of their own kind. To them they were all the same. The slimy arriving officers roughed his corpse around and stripped him of anything of value and never minded to search for evidence. Paula wanted answers. She called her girls at the hospital.

"Find out whatever you can and put me on point," she begged.

Whatever the girls could do, Paula would be the first to know, they agreed.

The truth and the smoking gun was never impossible to find in a jungle where fame and wealth was the avatar of life and death. Paula showed that cheese and rats crawled out of every hole with false and partially true names.

Rook's cousin Claud and his new protégé was at the top on her list. She had no idea who was Mr. Invisible Freddy-B, but blood thirsty Claud was a name the entire state of Missouri knew all too well. The fucked up part about it, he turned out to be Rook's relative.

Bad for Paula.

Claud had been busting ass in the Lou since Just Bleezy and the All Stars made their first video debut at the BET awards *Bitches Ain't All That.*

Even better, Paula's bitch, Diamond, was on an after-set black carpet picture with Yo Gotti and Claud back when he was doing security for the Kodak Center. Paula's plan was to copy the photo and have her man Boolue infiltrate the Rude Boy Mob and then tear it down brick by brick while she sat behind the curtain until her baby was born. Paula pained at the thought of bodying Peter. She refused to let that shit pass onto her seed while she was carrying her baby. There was little she could do. Her hands were tied. She had to let Boolue handle the situation his way. It was war time and Uncle James always knew to tuck his family first and burn every house until his enemies' blood rendered in mercy of the streets. She knew of an off grid honey comb hideout, which fell far from city blacks and Jamaicans.

Her home girl, Lil' Tina and Ty, posted up at her new home. Paula would only meet her girls at the Joplin, Missouri hotels and four star restaurants.

She could've had Scotty handle the whole beef though he was heavily affiliated.

On the other hand, her queen pin Diamond Assassin ego was far too stubborn and cocky to need another motherfucker handling her business, as she would put it.

Over the past four months a monstrous attack of automatic weapons sizzled throughout Hustle City in raindrops of AR-15 and SR-556 Ruger shells from Claud's flunkies and Paula's hot headed project crew going at it on sight.

Being that the Rude Boys busted at them first outside of Tead Drew's Ice Cream Shop on South Grand on some straight hoe shit about Lil' Monsta and Dead Head fucking all they hoes.

At Paula's consent, they took it to the Rude Boys. From both families the body count was crucial until they were ordered to get back to gettin' Paula's paper. The Rude Boys never let up.

Again, Paula had soon begun controlling paper spots on the darkside of South St. Louis, right under the Rude Boy's noses which allowed her to flip numbers three times higher. She was now copping 47 sections (kilograms) of coke by the time her supplier, Scotty, was moved to Memphis Prison Camp where she had bags dropped off for him. Hunted by a bloodhound guard named Doss, who spent hours hunting for cell phones and those who hit the gate to pick up bags and lay that wood on their wives at the motel a block away. Scotty called it

Camp Cupcake. Paula came that Friday to visit him. The visit went swell. Then she rested at the hotel.

At approximately 10 P.M., Scotty walked into Paula's motel room. She'd just finished showering. Scotty's eyes probed her full breast at a full peak as if they'd been fondled. Scotty's loins burned. He wanted this girl. Her pregnancy only made her that much more eatable.

Paula read his round eyes. She moved into his lust for the sake of getting more drugs only. He hadn't risked escape to be talking about more kilos though Paula was asking him to front her the amount she purchased. It was strictly business for her. He had been fresh with her each visit he required before she saw his people for more coke.

Scotty and Linda were history. She was sure of it. He made it clear that her sex would ace her request only. She swallowed her rejection of him and then helped him to pull his shirt off. He had man boobs and a plumber's body. He kicked away his dark grey sweats.

Her eyes fluttered at him disgustingly. His penis was small. It was rock hard with thick veins. She gripped it with a pull to lengthen it. Paula was a size queen like Janet. She kissed his neck and squalled, biting at her lower lip.

She'd never actually held a penis that felt like it was about to explode.

Her body winced before she inserted her fruity tongue into his mouth in pleasure as sex room played through her opened laptop glowing behind her.

He popped quickly.

Scotty thanked her for being thorough and breaking the friend code with Linda. If she were a boy, she would be under the real nigga code. Although he knew that business and sex never mixed. Scotty huge hands cuffed both of her thick chocolate cheeks. She mounted him, folding her caramel legs around his thick waist and eased the bulging head of his manhood onto her wet hole. Her arms enfolded his neck. Her head arched backwards. Paula whined as it opened her pussy to its peak. Scotty jabbed it in desperate strokes once again for round two. He was on Viagra.

"Damn, dis shit some heat!" he murmured as Paula's body began to do the pretty girl dip on him. Paula was having fun on it. After his first quick nut lubricated her, it was as if she was literally dancing on it now. His eyes blurred in tears. He felt good.

Her pregnancy kept her naturally wet. She sucked and nibbled at his left ear down to his shoulders. Scotty couldn't take it. His vein popped at each strike of her creamy muscle boning that meat. He stood Paula to her feet.

He laid his palms at the top of her dome. Her head followed his hand motion.

"Um'ma put this Bodu on num" she thought. She fell to her knees and stroked her neck slowly, allowing Scotty to enjoy a clear window seat of the best head he would ever receive. Paula was surgical with her head game. Her tongue moistened her lips and his dick at the same time. He grew weak as he gazed into her eyes. His scent was of her wetness. Her lips kissed over the head of it. Scotty's hook (cell phone) sounded on vibrate. It was an indication his time was up. He quickly gathered his clothes and headed back to the camp for the emergency census count.

CHAPTER SEVENTEEN – Cum Drink

Four days later... That day was one neither of them would ever forget. Paula felt the urge to kick it with her girls, Linda and Diamond. It was ladies night out so Linda suggested no men were allowed, other than Coop, who stuck to Paula like a wet tee shirt. Linda worked with her girl. She kept him occupied. She thought he had the coolest good boy gone bad swagger and brightest eyes, not to mention an exotic dancer build. Paula watched Diamond show the newly promoted Wet Diamond strippers how bitches in the 'Show Me' twerked that pole. She climbed to the top and dropped that thang, like Shardonay did on the Love of Ray J, without spilling a sip of her drink in hand. The lead stripper and veteran bottle poppers. "Wowed" in excitement to have such fun since their body blast trip, where birds roamed freely and gigantic turtles walked publicly over golden sanded beaches in El Salvador.

"My baby gone do it all!" Paula rubbed her belly watching Diamond wildn' out.

She was a bona fide professional freak around other lesbians. The other strippers gladly fondled her goodies and tasted her fresh bath and body from her sweat. Paula's cell buzzed. Coop brought it to her.

"Hold on," she spoke into her CEO office alone. She had food catered, free drinks, male and female dancers, a table of bamboo steamers with small Japanese dumplings nestled coyly inside and not to mention a girl friend of Linda's showed up with a new dish from her

Sweet and Savory Catering. As always, Knikki just had to be extra, she also brought everything they needed to accommodate their grown and sexy vibe. The club was literally Paula's from this night forward. She paid $200,000 for the joint in cold cash in both Linda and Diamond's good names with them being career medical personnel and small business owners. It worked.

"Hey, angel face!"

"Hey Scotty!" Paula's voice dragged behind Scotty's cough.

What happened at the telly was a hit and miss situation. It was nothing to take serious. Besides, the whole deal felt creepy to her. Fucking her close friend's ex beyond business purpose was her being ungrateful and slutty, Paula believed. Unaware that Linda and Scotty held a Will and Jada relationship, understanding and open. He snitched. But Linda knew the entire time. She respected Paula's moves. She knew Paula was a true hustler and had only done what any grinding bitch would do to get in with whales such as Scotty.

His type always seized what they desired. Linda's heart was long over her ex husband.

"Yeah. I heard about the death situation you going through and I feel yo' pain, lil' sista. It's situations like that, I spoke to you about the day we did our first business. Like I said, death is a part of this business and you must have the stomach to face it head on regardless of whose turn it is to get it. Ain't nothing promised, but what you live and you die by."

At his words, Paula glanced out of her office mirror tinted window at Linda's face smashed into Coop's cheek. He enjoyed it. Linda was a hot piece that could steal any man's attention.

"I'm sorry for your loss," he lied in speaking of Tearence..

"I know that he's in a better place where he'll get the care and love that's required from the Almighty. You best trust he is in great company with Biggie and many other soul legends so to speak." Scotty was full of shit. He killed and destroyed men he thought Linda was close to. King rich and territorial was one thing Paula peeped of him, but had to respect certain othere things about him.

He always held a great conversation and said the right things at the oddest times. A bit creepy, but she felt a lash of joy for him every time they'd spoken whether she wanted to listen or not. What he had to say, he was going to say it regardless.

"You know, Pauli, I may not of told you, but the minute you left that county jail holdover years ago, I've done my homework on you. I knew your mom!"

Paula held her right breast and reclined her black and pink Prada leather office chair. "How you know my mother?"

Scotty stepped away from the rec yard into the open woods, cautiously to prevent being caught using his cell phone in prison. If caught, he'd face up to twelve additional months. He had inmates posted from R&D to A-Unit's counselor's office on look out. His money was long and everyone wanted a piece of it, including a dirty cop named Bryant who tipped him off when he ran out to obtain a bag.

"Yeah, Pauli, everybody wanted to know ya' old bird after she hit-up them two crackers with that chainsaw."

Paula denied such.

"Well that's sure how they described it in The World Newspaper!"

Paula stared into the mist of her office interior that he even spoke of her mom. She said nothing.

He continued, "Oh, you know my Italian rappy here corresponds with Pam's celly as we speak."

Paula teared up. "Have you spoken to her recently?" She fished.

"By the way, yes, the other day now that you mention it. She called my sister. We kicked it on a party line." He smiled with his cell pressed to his face in secret as he returned to his housing unit. He rested calmly on the toilet. "You know she mentioned she was sick, that she wanted to be around her family and if she couldn't transfer closer to home, then she wanted to be closer to her children," he lied making convo. "I never mentioned I knew you," he added.

"Did she mention my sister Carla passing away?"

"No, but she did mention that she lives on inside of you and you always been there for her even when other people shitted on na. And for you to stand tall and be proud of being the great daughter that you are and she wished you would thank God for the time that he has allowed us both with a good loving and God fearing soul."

Most of it he lied about.

Scotty had returned to his cubicle for count. He ended the call without any notice. Paula wanted to thank him for his words. They lifted her spirits.

She slid her office laptop closer to her. Her swift fingers rattled across the small black keys fast. It read,

"My morning will last 'til the days dwindle by and my sorrow will go on and on, for my unborn daughter's beloved father. But the memories and respect for you, I'll cherish as the beating of my heart. I already miss your wisdom and strength. I will continue to hold you down your entire bid as family during your silent spiritual transformation. In closing, today is the reflection of yesterday, today and tomorrow."

Love Pauli

Smile! Photos are on the way as of now of tonight's event. Don't worry big bro, I got these hos sitting on Moe bottles. That work is for you. Get the fella's that ain't afraid to hit that fence that got plenty of big faces on deck. You just line 'em up and ma hoes gonna knock 'um down. I'll be sure to bring the ones of your picking. Don't worry, I got um all flavors.

L.O.L. #-Pound.

She closed her text with a smile and returned to her guest after emailing her mother inquiring of her relationship with a Scotty Myers.

The whole time Pam was lost behind those creepy ass bars in Chillicothe Women's Missouri State Prison serving twenty years for two bodies, she never questioned Paula once on how she was known. Suddenly, now able to take care of herself and send her money every month and that she pulled up in a new whip each time she showed her face on the prison's parking lot where Pam stood early morning with other women that she had a beef with or had to put hands on for some bitch talk about what her baby girl was said to of been out there doing which wasn't their damn business. The rumors were always spread by bitches that came in with fresh sentences. The new girls were the ones pressured into sex acts with the big boned butch chicks that ran portions of the prison yard.

Pam was cellies with Scotty's brother's ex-wife Stacy, that he forced to take the fall for six kilo's of coke coming from Scotty and Linda's cafe in Lake St. Louis. Big Stacy kept it one hundred with Pam about who Scotty really was and that Linda had always been a sweetheart who would take care of Paula if she liked her. Pam was grateful for the info, but would've never trusted neither of them split licking hoes for as far as she could throw them. As far as she was concerned, it was only two real bitches in her mind and one happened to be a picture of her deceased baby girl, Carla who's face was on her left breast and the one she prayed every night for othere than the photo on her pink ID card. She wasn't about to get caught up into those lil young, simple minded lost bitches fake dick and pussy fuck games. She felt she was too grown for that shit. Besides, Big Stacy had no idea Pam had got the scoop from some white bitches that Pam played close for shit she needed done unaccessible to black inmates and that the white girls hated the same hoes she despised. They exposed Stacy's closest secret of her getting fucked with cucumbers and sucking off Black Betty and C-Swift during chow in the chapel building. Pam wished that bitch would look at her sideways.

Stacy never crossed that line with her hearing Pam speak on gutting one of those hoes if they'd ever disrespected her womanhood.

Pam stayed to herself and secretly talked to her baby girl late nights from her cell phone when certain guards were on duty.

CHAPTER EIGHTEEN – The Chameleon

Boolue slid through Cook Avenue on point and on schedule as Paula had planned. Boolue was skilled at connecting the dots. He was born a Chameleon. Since Tearence's death, he began peeping everyone who was known as a big time stunna. Selling half's and whole grams for $30 and $60 of some shit they'd stepped on twice already. He investigated the situation from the Blue Myers to Wellston and found only one soul that he gladly picked apart for the truth. Black Randy was his grand target whom happened to be twisted by them letter boys (F.B.I.) and plus his janky-ass admired Boolue and there suggested he leave the block questioning deadly circumstances of Tearences's slaying.

All lips were paid, sealed and sworn silence to the Rude Boy Family. Besides, Freddy-B had babbling soldiers everywhere and tentacles like a squid. Randy keyed Boolue on point and explained to him the risk of trying to reach out to the Raster Family over what the hood called, "spilled milk."

The Jamaicans loved to kill. They whacked babies and all. In war there are always casualties. No one mattered. They had that mula and countless blood hounds who were willing to slap Sarah Palin at a presidential debate for a quarter brick of the mountain size crunchy white dog food (heroin) the Rude Boys supplied throughout Hustle City and East St. Louis. 83rd was the Rude Boy's sworn code of honor. At this time, Boolue had played it 007 and used the Rude Boy's weakest link, Randy, as a mole. It was the only way he could blend into the hood where he schemed to assassinate them brick by brick and Paula from afar watched them crumble down to her nemesis Freddy-B, who stood in her way of being the first Hustle City Madam.

Paula's main plan was to steal Freddy-B's connect in Queens along with his life.

She was heartless. This lick would unfold her wildest dreams and grant her and Boolue presidential paper. Tearence would definitely get the reburial he would have wanted with an elephant tusk Gucci tomb near the Florida Keys where his family, all except his cousin Trina and Lavell, moved away to after his assassination. Boolue muscled Randy into plugging him with the Rude Boy Family.

Although Randy had american guts, brilliantly, this fool could remember most of his childhood in Kingston. He was able to pop royal names from the top of his head of Kingston to the burrough of Queens, N.Y. as if he had stood side by side with the legends. He was afraid of Boolue, but terrified of the 'Great Scorpion', Freddy-B. Randy agreed with a hug. "Be careful, 'ma' dude. Dim don't take no sho't," said the unborn Rasta Randy. "I'll plug you killa, but me don't want a thing to do with you after the fire is burning in your soul." The Rude Boy's had Randy spooked like Screw Face in the movie, *Marked for Death*.

"So, what happened to that pistol case you caught 8 months ago?" Boolue asked as he dialed out to Paula's smart phone.

Whenever Randy was lying, or nervous, the nigga would come out of him. "Shid man, I got me a lawyer on that shit. I got scott-free. He took care of that shit, hommy. You feel me?" Randy's voice trembled in a hood tone. He lied.

Boolue peeped game.

"Yeah!" Randy responded as Boolue's primed out 99 K-5 truck yanked from the heat of the curb.

Freddy B's cartel had flipped nearly 200 sections (kilos) of heroin during the last few weeks. His bill counter clogged due to accumulated residue from the thousands of crispy big faces. Some of which smelled of unbathed junkies as if they'd been pulled out of somebody's ass.

Freddy-B was given word that a drought was about to pop off. He was swinging at 500 sections this re-up. Cook had turned into one of his most blessed trap spots since the slaughter of Tearence. Literally, every hundred blocks was on fire. You could hardly tell the true Rastas from the born St. Louisian. Everyone from the crummy hood was either sporting twisters or rocking dreads. The dope the jamaicans were putting down was so potent and plentiful, vet smokers such as Geesta, Muff, and other closet smokers either OD'd or posted up flipping halves and wholes with doe boy knots in their pockets spitting babies and talking cash shit about nothing. The words recession held no barrens for the dope game. The punishment was reduced to 18 to 1 for crack dealers. Obama had finally put something in play for the black man, seeing that he saw some forms of unfairness compared to powdered coke and crack.

On a bright Monday evening, a well feared stick up boy named Dee Dee slid through Cook only to cop a few grams of white heroin to snort. Dee Dee had pulled up to the curb in a powder blue Delta, then, as he trotted from Ms. Thomas' gangway and got in his car. Jackie Boy put a crease in his ass, a clear warning for all jack boys not to even ride though C.A. (Cook Avenue). Jackie Boy then kicked Dee

Dee's limp body over to the passenger seat and sped away dumping his corpse behind the Y.M.C.A. on Page and Montclair Ave. Home of the B.O.D.'s'

By the time Freddy-B's new work landed a day before the first of the month, the Rude Boys were responsible for six more bodies and the home invasion of a brutal palm slapping one of Cook Ave's own, light skinned Keyshia for gossiping about how everybody let the Jamaicans take over C.A. after murking the big homies, Tearence. She was pissed and hoped Paula gutted these blood suckers. The usual punishment for breaking silence and secret meant death, but Claud spared Keyshia's red ass. He was busting them guts on the reg.

At this moment in the game, it had been almost a full month since the death of Tee. Boolue had excelled rank in the Rude Boy brotherhood. Fabricated loyalty and a cold heart was his gifted asset passed on through his genes from his father, Black Mark. You know they say, "all the real gangstas are dead and gone!' and that's exactly where Boolue's father lay.

It was easier said than done, of how Boo made it to be the Rude Boy's lieutenant by holding onto Randy's coat tail. Being that Boolue lived through the eyes of his monstrous street reputation, he was revealed to Freddy-B as a paper getting fearless goon with nothing better to live for. He'd already closed out three hits for the brotherhood. Little did they know, Boolue was reporting to Paula and responsible for kicking down Claud's lieutenant's trap house door and pinning him and his jamaican queen, Coochi to their kitchen wall with a 200 round, fully auto .45 caliber Commando just two weeks prior.

Paula's plan was working swell.

On top of Boo getting rich, Paula's pussy was wet with vindictive passion.

She'd subdued the wealth and luxury street cred she aimed for. For her, there was more. It was as if the more paper she stacked, the more diabolical her traumatized mind became unrealistically drawn to wealth.

In some ways, at times, she found herself living in an inception, not clear of what world was real. Her love for a mother who was doing a twenty year bid and sister who was long gone was the only balance that kept her sane.

Boolue himself bent over backwards to prove his false diligence to Freddy-B, in which at the moment, he was blinded by the material fullness of a rich man's life of price tags that never seemed to fulfill his crazy gut feeling to escape the shackles of the streets in which he sometimes questioned his own loyalty for Paula's $250K hit that he was sworn to. Unlike the rest of the hood, they took for granted that Boolue had fallen into the bubble of the blood money Rude Boy Claud had showered throughout Hustle City. The Rude Boys were making more noise dropping off bodies and winning over the streets through fear.

Paula hated it! Even though she hasn't missed a beat getting her paper, the strip joint and her new ballroom located on Cherokee, (The Casablanca Ballroom) had taken over the party life of the Lou. Not to mention the 120K, plus the P.J.'s clocked in weekly.

The Rude Boys had different faces back and forth from Harlem to Kingston and back to Missouri killing their rivals. In a few situations, dirty cops that pushed up on the bloody mob for hush money were quickly eliminated in gunfire.

May 14, Boolue's 2/10 Lambo style ultra indigo colored Lexus unfolded the parking lot of Dave & Buster's in St. Louis West County, seating his two beautiful twin daughters, Alanta and Alexis. Being it was Father's Day, spending time with his two favorite ladies was essential. To his surprise, the ticket to his soul mission had pulled up beside him at a red light just before highway 70's east entrance.

"Damn, that's ma dude Scott-free!" Boolue mumbled as his twin girls sat side by side at his right playing X-Box 360 Call of Duty video game. Boolue downed his platinum tinted window. He waved for the Attoneys attention. The two men were all too well acquainted. They pulled onto the nearest Walgreen's lot. Boolue had a few must know questions. The well respected high class attorney denied any dealings with a Randy Gilbert. It was obvious the kid lied and was possibly working with the government. The Attorney explained how the case had turned fedz on a 921(B) with the conditions of 851 enhancements for the only Randy he knew. Boolue hit the well dressed attorney palm with the six hundred bucks he had as pocket change. Boo furthered his day to meet with the twins mother, Ingram in Lake St. Louis to get blessed the rest of the holiday with some Father's Day lips, hips and jawbone that Ingram took pride in pleasing her man.

The very next morning as Boo was about to pull from his new townhome, that he coped in his bitch name under a tax lien certificate. The place had only needed cosmetic work. Boolue knew the mission and the goons he was fucking with took what chu loved when you violated. There wasn't any second chances dealing with these fools. Boolue thought ahead of the game. He tucked his love ones far off into

St. Louis county and ordered wifey to stay out of the city unless it was on some official business downtown. He rested his eyes over his wifey laying across their queen sized bed naked with a Zyion Jay-Z blue silk sheets drawn between her open legs lodged into her petite ass cheeks exhausted behind the crushing Boo had put down last night. He tucked his 40 into his black Rocawear book bag on top of a brick and ½ of heroin. The holiday was over. It was back to business Paula paid him to do. He took off in Ingram's 2012 black Diamond Infiniti wearing factory chrome 22 inch Rucci Rims. Ringtone by Akon and Alica Keys, *Ghetto Story*, Boolue pressed a silver button located at the center of his steering wheel. He answered.

"Yeah mond Claud!" Was all Claud needed to say. His voice was official. That alone meant, "Get that paper to the house!" And everyone who dealt with the Rude Boys responded to it as so.

"Trey's-up" Boolue yelled into the interior of his Infiniti in which indicated he was in route. He then disconnected and immediately dialed out to Randy's cell. Like usual, Randy's hands were filled. He was pinned to his set loving the fact Tina's head being buried in his lap in a top row corner seat at a Rams Vs. Washington NFL game at the Edward Jones Dome.

"Me busy mond. Call me later."

Randy shouted through Boolue's surround sound as he exited onto Grand Boulevard. "Fool, miss me with that phony ass accent! I just checked with my people about that case yo ass caught, nigga. You know what they told me, don't chu?"

Boolue frowned.

Randy removed Tina from his lap and stepped away for privacy. "Hold on Boo man. What chu mean, I know?" He boggled.

Boolue's husky voice hammered his ears. "Yell, fuck boy, game's over. I'm up on yo ass! Nigga, yo' ass hot! You workin' a deal with them people."

Randy stood there frozen at the truth as he continued.

"But I tell you what hot boy. We both gon' gain from this. You with that?" Boolue asked.

Randy stuttered. "Ye...yeah. So what chu want from me?" the rat asked pitifully.

"You know, Rude Boy. It's simple. Introduce me to Mr. Invisible and then forget I even knew yo hot ass fuck boy." Boolue took a spit out of his window to rid the bad taste that he ever spoke to that rat.

"A'ight Rude Boy. You got that, but first you got to pull the impossible,"

Randy claimed.

"Yeah, and what's that fool?"

"You got to make the Black Mamba disappear and then I'll introduce you to Freddy-B as his new animal," Randy added. "We'll call you the Scorpion."

Randy's eyes widened as if he spoke words of magic.

"Man, why the fuck you just can't introduce me by ma name? That ain't ma damn hand cock!" Boo hissed.

"Because the great Jaguar believes in reading one's soul," Randy assured Boolue.

"Yeah, aight, whatever. Just text me Claud's address and I'll gladly handle that ass ASAP fool!"

Click.

CHAPTER NINETEEN - Cross

"These mother fuckers must do read minds!" Boolue thought as he parked across the ravine on Cook Avenue watching Claud and four of his flunkies smoking some purple flowers that Boolue's keen nose sensed THC floating through his A/C vents as his engine rested. Every time Boo met with Claud's Akon black dreaded ass, his dick jumped. He wanted to put seventeen into his sappy dreads. As Boolue jogged toward Wonny's third floor apartment where he had Claud's 88 stack sat 44 a section. He tossed his book bag across his shoulder and winked at Woony's daughter, Red, another glitch occurred.

"Bumba Clot, see me Rude Boy!" said Claud forcefully as the slick headed brown skin rasta tapped Claud's shoulder.

"Dead him mond!"

Boolue thought little of it. He eased his stride over to Claud's black on black 2-10 Audi. Boolue informed Claud that he was dirty and would meet him at Wonny's spot. Claud insisted he chill a few seconds, that he had him faded if the Jump Out Boys slid up. Claud assured palming two of the nastiest chrome Desert Eagles with a sly smile followed in laughter from his passengers.

"Claud, you're one crazy Jamaican. So what, I guess yo' crazy ass gone blast it out with the one times?" Boolue's dry voice asked.

"I'll shoot it out with me God," said Claud

Lil Tom's raspy voice thundered from the top step of the open walkway. "Boolue, watch out homie!" Lil Tom upped. His Glock fired in pursuit toward the ramping gun fire crackling like bricks of Black Cat fire crackers on the Fourth of July that splattered from the speeding 2010 BMW Z-4 hard top convertible. Fully auto uzi shots made love to the three story building, hunting for bodies, especially Boolue's! The gold Beemer aggressively cut a sharp left onto Cook from Jones Avenue, seating two freshly trimmed brown completed late 20's men, possibly Latino, who looked from the outer state. Boolue dropped his bag and sprinted behind several parked cars in front of Claud's Audi. Claud peeled rubber seconds after the shots began without firing a single round as he promised he would. Lil Tom was struck twice in the abdomen and left shoulder. His gut instinct prevented Boolue from being judged by two and carried by six.

Lil Tom was quickly hoisted into Cortez's first floor apartment and later admitted to St. Louis University Hospital and released the following two days. He was pissed.

The whole time Boo chilled at the crib with Ingram A.K.A. Pokerhonus. She was a big girl, fine to death with three master degrees from the State of Kentucky. Boolue was home figuring out the bittersweet behind the attempt on his life in which he solely explained to his boss, Paula, being that Claud had stalled him in the middle of the streets all that time besides the fact he had 88K to pick up and not to mention his crazy ass never let loose one round, as he promised to 'shoot it out with God.'

An urban female Big Noon had a bird's eye view from her third floor window.

She put Boolue up on game. She had a crush on Boolue. The killing part was that it seemed even more lopsided. Claud bragged about having wheelchair Scrappy to put down a hit nearly identical six weeks ago on Rockaway Boulevard in Queens, New York. Even better, the most spooky part in his situation, a while back Boo had spoken to black Randy of bodying Claud's ugly ass and even worse, hood niggaz never do drive bys in $57,000 whips. Boolue went over the pieces with Ms. Paula. She quickly put them together.

"Handle what you're paid to do," said the Big Cahoona.

Boolue later swam beside his twins. Either way, it was time for Claud to meet the reaper.

Later the next morning, Claud had been calling Boo's cell like an abandoned hoe. He wanted to know what was on his mind about the shooting after the fact he missed his target. Even worse, Freddy-B's bald headed vicious ass inquired about the 88 stacks that were riding on Claud's neck. Serendipity, the fuck boy Randy, couldn't of come through at any more of an awkward time. The worm was still on the hook.

Boolue took notice. Randy's photo covered his touch dial screen as a missed call number. Boo hit him right back. Ringtone Toni Braxton sounded. Boo thought queer of Randy's ringtone.

"Yeah, what's up Boo? I can't talk, bro, but here's the address you asked for. Florissant County, 3970 Max Weich Place. Oh, there's a teenage girl and a snow bunny there, you feel me?"

"Are you sure that's yo' word?" Boo checked.

"Is an elephant heavy?" Randy sarcastically responded.

"Damn, these fuck boys these days sound like real street niggaz," Boo groused.

As expected, the sound of a detective radio sounded. Boolue clicked off knowing that fool was in shit up to his knees fucking with them letter boys. It's time to handle that business. He swore as he dressed. Listening to *In the Club* by 50 Cent that displayed from their small Boss system in their kitchen where Ingram readied his and the twin's breakfast.

Boolue contacted Lil Tom offering him a piece of the Rude Boy's ass that they both felt an itch to scratch. "I'll slide through in an hour big Homie, Boolue promised.

Nearly thirty minutes away in Florissant County, far from Mayberry, the small subdivision was upscale and owned by rich whites and silver spoon fed blacks. The classic Uncle Tom, to say. Claud lay there in a $314,900 white sided bricked four bedroom home. The sun beamed overhead as Ziggy pulled her Derion summer hat over her forehead dressed in a scarlet Ruched convertible strapless cross-back dress matching a pair of Christian Loubutin fishnet cork stilettos. As Ziggy entered her home, she was greeted by her mix daughter's father, Rude Boy Claud butt ass naked holding an AR-15 with a hard dick staring into her devil blue eyes.

Ziggy smiled and yelled out to her man, "What gwan do?"

She dropped her Macy's bag sensually unveiling her clothing, bearing her 40D-28-36 nude Caucasian Hungarian skin covered with punk rock fire orange Derion heels hugging her matching toenails.

Claud tossed his AR-15 onto his leather Gucci recliner and stepped to his bitch ravishing his tongue rough over her sexually entertained nipples like an algae fish.

Ziggy was an established V.P. and state director for T.I.M.S. Kidney and Breast cancer affairs. This European diva was a noble citizen at sunrise and a Rasta dick bandit by night. She moaned and motioned herself to their wood frame bed where she enjoyed spreading her palms across the edge of the smooth framing. She aggressively guided Claud's 7 ¾ inch muscle into her trimmed cunt with exotic moans as she quickly bagged it up on him like a city girl. She fucked him raw dog.

Claud was pleased as usual. Ziggy always put on for her Rude Boy king. She thought there was nothing better than pleasing her king. In her mind, he was that and she was no more than a crummy potter's daughter sent to win his highness' favor. Ziggy boned him in slow motion for minutes on.

Claud shouted in pleasure, "Crucial ting, blood clot!" He drummed deeper into her creaming hole in lust. Both of their bodies dripped in unyielding sweat from nearly two hours of autonomous Tyrese love making like Superhead and Mr. Marcus. He stood holding Ziggy's silky legs hung over his forearms as her thin back side laid creased in the V of their bedroom wall taking as much dick as her warm wet hole would engulf.

Claud was packin'. The way he worked it felt good to Ziggy's camel toe.

Her sex was white girl wild. She isolated him until she was able to mount an unbalanced stance with her long golden hair draped over her sweaty shoulders. Her tan skin scented of Bond #9 New York Brooklyn fragrance as she kneeled and offered her man into the frame of her wet throat.

The Rude Boy stared down into his sex slave's submissive vixen blue eyes lined in a gold get'em girl Bobby Brown eyeliner as she gazed at his muscular hips, thrust his thickness into the walls of her jaw. His manly sex slipped back and forth at the base of her thick throat as he slowly leveled to his toes, which only ignited Ziggy's juices.

She palmed his huge testicles with her right hand as her left jerked at the core of his rocket. Her soft tongue exercised his shaft greedily giving him that Rude Girl Becky at full throttle, subconsciously knowing Claud wanted another round of her pink wet-wet. His grip tightened at the hook of her in utopia excited by her painful squints. His animal was released.

He boned Ziggy as if he'll never see her again to the sounds of Alica Keys and Maxwell's *Fire We Make*. This was by far the best dick Claud had given Ziggy since their first encounter. Wherever his torturous explosion came from, in Ziggy's book, it didn't matter as long as he kept that fire dick stroking her G spot. She came multiple times.

As Claud's whiskey stained lips tugged at her dark rigid nipples, he took repeated backward steps causing her raw knees to follow his knee bending movements to reserve the chunky feel roaming her wet mouth in ecstasy.

Claud was angry. He knew at this moment he had to finish what he started and sex wasn't what he insinuated. He had to judge Boolue by six in the worst way for disrespecting his Don Dada. Having Freddy-B to question him about a punk ass eighty-eight stacks. Claud had never come short with a package. Lateness showed signs of weakness and he wasn't having that on his watch. All he knew was that Boolue was about to be one dead nigga as soon as he got done blowing Ziggy's back out. He stood Ziggy to her tip toes and slid his trunk into her pre-cum laced cunt. She stretched her thirsty neck toward his. She zig-zagged her long wet tongue over his tatted shoulder and tightened her cunt muscle over his bone.

"Rude Boy. Yes me Claud!" Ziggy moaned as the sound of breaking glass sounded over Claud's husky, thrusting grunts.

"Hold on baby, what was that noise?" Ziggy inquired pausing her grind while peeking over Claud's shoulder toward their locked second floor bedroom door.

"That's me cat," said Claud. Lying Ziggy face down on their bed, he put every inch of him into her vibrating, orgasming hole.

"Get dis pussy!" Ziggy screamed, taking spits at Claud's strokes as it ascended from her taste.

"Wone spit on it Ziggy!" said Claud. He loved it when her freak came out.

There was no telling what Ziggy would do during a sexual encounter.

"Momma's cumming!" she yelled.

Claud drilled harder, faster and lengthily. Whiteness oozed around his stiff meat going in and out of her. Their passion rose, the room scented of her body wash more than ever.

A sinister of love covered them as their bedroom door echoed a heavy knock followed by the sound of Ziggy's white mother who came by to visit.

"Claud, open this door now!" she shouted in a fueled voice.

Claud tugged at Ziggy to rid her old bird (mother) until they'd dressed properly. Boolue and Lil Tom had come to do a job regardless of who had to get it. Ziggy's mother, Jennifer Carter had unseated her black and silver 2/11 Buick Lacrosse. The woman was apprehended by two masked gunmen. Before she could muster another breath to scream, the huge man wearing black class one wheat Timbo boots, faded jeans and a black mask covering his face stuffed the barrel of his 12 gauge into the cavern of her mouth with force, splitting her shit. Blood ran down from her broken tooth.

"Bitch, don't say a damn word. You holla, I swear I'll make this gauge sing to yo' old ass," he promised.

She shook her head in complete agreement with the two assailants by a careful nod tasting the gun powder from the previous fired open barrel. She was terrified.

"Now, slowly again. Where is Claud?" Boolue asked, walking her old ass into the home.

She let him in with her spare key. She then told them, "I'm not even sure if he is here!"

"I see now old bitch. You think this is a motherfuckin' game? Bitch, stop lying! I seen all of his fucking cars parked out front," the masked man whispered as his eyes searched curiously through the narrow hallway.

Lil Tom's huge palm violated her white skin with force. Her body plunged against the wall deplacing a family photo which smashed onto a cherry wooden junk mail stand.

The sound of glass echoed.

Jennifer took the two men to her son-in-law's demise, hoping her beloved granddaughter and daughter weren't home. Either way, it was a fucked up situation which caused Ziggy's mom to knock on their bedroom door in the first place.

After she ordered the door to be opened, Ziggy responded standing to her pink painted toes tying her gold hair into a pony. "Mom, why are you constantly banging on my damn door like you've lost your mind?" Ziggy shouted, dressing.

Claud laid there wishing her old ass would stop cock blocking. Claud knew her mother hated the fact her precious daughter was solely in love and was being ruled by a vicious Jamaican that deep down she harbored a sick fantasy of hittin' that chocolate meat herself.

Ziggy's mom was an old cougar. She yelled in sounds of tears as Lil Tom held the barrel of his gauge underneath Jennifer's Liz Claiborne skirt up the crack of her tight, flat ass.

"Ziggy, open this door damn it. I mean it, right now. Open the door please!"

she shivered.

"For what? What's wrong Mom?" Ziggy asked.

Boolue's patience was wearing on him. He threatened to now kill everyone in the spot if Claud's greasy ass didn't show his face.

Claud flared. "Woomp Boy! Bumba Clot, what gwan Jenny? Bag off me door?"

The sounds of Claud's Jamaican voice sent wooping butterflies through Lil Tom's healing wounds. For all he knew, this bumba clot had him hit up. Lil Tom's fidget thick fingers handcuffed his trigger. Boolue was done playing cat and mouse with this pussy. Lead by Boolue's AK-47, the assassins forced their way into the room as Ms. Jennifer laid face down with her ass up praying to God at the sight of the huge masked men.

Ziggy stood, deplaced in her thoughts. "What the fuck?" She cursed as her dear mother reached out to the men, in gagging tears, for their sympathy not to execute her child.

Claud quickly reached for his Desert Eagle pistol from the side of his Whirlpool mattress. "Rude Boy!" He shouted, fueling himself for war or sudden death.

Claud was trained for this moment. Hell was about to break loose.

Despite Boolue's mask, Claud paid attention to his body build and facial features. He knew it was Boolue holding the AK rifle. The two men never once broke eye contact. Neither of them cared about dying. Today was a special day. It was blessed with honor, revenge, pride, two beautiful women and a mountain size table of raw, uncut heroin.

This was the perfect dog fight. Long to of come. Clearly, a love hate spectrum brewing and Boolue definitely had the right ingredients. Ziggy dove to the floor as Claud screamed. He pulled his forearm from under the bed.

"You die!" The Rasta yelled gripping his Desert.

Boolue followed by Lil Tom. The boys isolated the situation, leaving Rude Boy Claud's entire forearm severed from his slant body crumbled at the side of his night stand.

Claud's mother in law and fiancée wasn't injured.

Days later, that evening, the world read, Ms. Ziggy and her mother, Mrs.

Jennifer Carter arrived home approximately 4:11pm and discovered Claud Rashad Odyssey, Jr.'s deceased body, armless with Timberland boot prints muffed over his face. The home had no obvious missing items or showed any signs of foul play by the family. Ms. Carter and Ziggy figured Claud had messed up some of Freddy-B's drugs and he called a hit on Claud. Ziggy was wrong! Florissant homicide detective, Michael Newberry had confirmed Claud's brutal homicide. That it had shook the entire community, reported to be drug related. It was an open and closed case.

Now the Rude Boy family was pissed.

Freddy-B decided behind Randy's word alone to promote Boolue, the Scorpion, as his new enforcer. Mr. Invisible had one thing on his mind. Some mother fucker had violated his royal family and it was time to put the fear of God into the entire state of Missouri.

CHAPTER TWENTY – Killing Sprees

May 27, 2014 the St. Louis Evening World read as, "Violence rattles city and county statewide over multiple weekends. In the Walnut Park district a massive blood bath robbed nine men of their lives in the 5400 block of Wren Avenue near Robin Avenue. The shooting lasted nearly fourteen minutes before the 9th District Police arrived to find AR-15 casing voyaging from the murder scene to almost half a block. Bullet holes covered 5423 Wren where Fat Chris and Mook Loc, two neighborhood residents were slaughtered by a spray of shots from what survivors said, came from a rampaging masked man that moved in and out like the reaper claiming the nine lives before he was chained by a silver 2009 Gran Turismo Maserati. In other news, homicide detectives discovered another gruesome scene near Cardinal Glenert Hospital on South Grand and Park Avenue. Two lay slain inside a home where a police spokesman told gawkers at the scene that they had responded to reports of shots fired. Upon arrival, detective Danny found a black couple executed.

Bean Pole Williams and an unidentified female cuddled in a Bridgestone wooden bed, soaked in a pool of fire, smoke and burned blood, which ran from Bean Pole's corpse, partially bound, to the unknown victim's burned skull. The major Case Unit argued that all three executions were related based on the shell casings found, though there were discrepancies of Claud's killing.

Freddy B gave no one immunity. Everyone Claud dealt first hand with. The Great Jaguar whacked!

With every muscle within his reach, Hustle City had to feel the terror of the Bumba Clot kingpin. Like Lucifer, Boolue stayed in his ear and at his side in a few cases feeding him lies, pointing fingers at other Rude Boys he gave no fuck about. Boolue was as wicked as they came. Freddy-B was turning in circles answering Boolue's prayers claiming the lives of his own street family. Black Randy being on the bottom of his hit list. A sense of victory began to roam Freddy-B's heart.

"One out of those bodies was Claud's assassin!" Boolue lied. The two men rendered themselves in closeness.

Freddy-B was sleeping with an enemy. There was one mistake he'd made besides allowing Boolue to weasel his way so close to him. Freddy-B had never chosen his general at random before.

There was another fragment Freddy-B missed.

Jamaican Ron from Robin Avenue was plugged with his Rude Boy connect in Queens, NY. Big Ron took flight out to Queens, NY and delivered word that Freddy- B's situation had rats. Big Ron had moles within the STL's law enforcement field. Ron expressed the turbulence of his diligence to the source Bullet.

The president of Kill Point crime family declared a 10 million dollar hit to be placed on Freddy-B's head immediately. He was going to be dealt with during his next re-up. Bullet planned the hit due to Big Ron's word that the C.I. was lurking within the Rude Boys Fole. Bullet felt bad about the fact he had to whack his old Rasta brother. It was business, never personal.

Regardless, at all means he had to clean up the shit before it reached his business associates in Kingston. By the time the 15th rolled around, Freddy- B was now being accompanied by his next top killer to re-up with him. There was no telling what corner a large drug transaction would turn. Shit got ugly at a drop of a dime when them big boy figures came to play. The Rude Boy weren't taking no chances. As he figured, anybody could get it.

Freddy-B had the right motherfucker at his side. Boolue lived by that code.

Mr. Invisible arranged to score 5,000 pounds this trip. The city hadn't seen that much dope since Aurther Qualls was on the throne.

After the Bomba Clot killing spree, fools from Cape Girardeau to Charleston were dropping paper off to Boolue that they'd owed Claud. Niggaz were terrorized. They thought Claud's spirit was putting that work in. Freddy-B used the

AR-15 for that specific reason. It was Claud's custom tool besides his twin Deserts.

Heading into here another hot summer on a warm sunny day of June. Everything but peace settled in the city of the lost Angels. California had the weight of the world binding on the shoulders of the Los Angeles Lakers for the NBA Western Conference Championship. Tied at 83, the Phoenix Suns bench and their hundreds of fans fell silent as Byron Scott and his Lakers took a demanding 22 point lead going into halftime.

Freddy-B and Boolue gassed up Freddy-B's black cherry private helicopter lined with a platinum landing gear. The men flew out to attend the game using seasonal seat tickets. It was the one thing beside

Jamaican football the Great Jaguar used to relax.

Boolue soaked in every moment as if he was living one of his dreams. It was his first trip out of the Missouri region. His bottom bitch Ingram had been watching the news for the last five days. She was horrified though Boolue hadn't called once. His mind was on Paula's situation, he stuck by Freddy-B like flies on shit. Each body they found veered closer to the vicinity of her man's whereabouts. His unreturned presence and the more bodies found only increased Ingram's anxiety. Her patience had expired just as her beautiful twins walked in from school. She met them at the front door and seated into her lovers ultra indigo two door Lexus heading into the city in search for him despite his wishes ordering her to stay out of the city limits.

The well dressed Jamaicans were excited. He swiped his black Visa Rush card. Drinks for his entire fifty seat section at his disposal one row from court side behind the Phoenix Sun's bench. The two men slapped palms. Rubbed elbows and blew some of LA's finest kush. Boolue copped on Cali's own 74th street.

They kicked it as if they were frat brothers. Boolue was the best at befriending the high maintenance type. He knew what they wanted and catered to them with a forced smile.

This was his best kept secret. The boy was a hundred forty four thousand bucks richer from the reaps of his half of the heroin he and Lil Tom kidnapped from Claud's home. Boo sold his end whole, for the 144 to a hustlin' ass diva named Tommy from Kintlock. The rest of Claud's merch was left behind by the boys. They were in and out in a snap.

Ziggy and her conniving mother broke down the back door and pried open his safe. His jewelry and $6,000 in cash was attacked by the girls. They moved back to Queens and opened a Five Season Multi Culture diva boutique on Jamaica Boulevard. It became very successful.

In which damn surely, Jennifer hoped happen long before now. Her daughter was finally freed from Claud's asphalt black ass. She celebrated during their whole flight to the Big Apple.

For a split second, Freddy-B's company occupied the void that burned where Boolue's soul used to be. He was the one type who drove an all black Benz and an iced out Jesus piece with an atheist belief.

Considerably, he was the walking dead in her eyes. Boolue and Rook always fantasized about being caked up and living life beyond. Despite Rook dying by the hands of his most trusted pottna. No one knew. Boolue would do anybody for cash. He mimicked a Hustle City legend named CoCo who was the rawest in the hit man game since Sammy the Bull was tore off.

Tears cornered Boolue's glazed eyes for the first time in his life. He realized the amount of street cred he obtained, plus people loved the way the new Queen looked out. Everyone was given their just due until they burned their own asses with her.

Boolue excused himself for a beverage. Now is the time to break his neck, Boolue contemplated seriously. He stared at the back of Freddy-B's bald head as he sat there enjoying the curvaceous performance of the Harajuku Barbie, Nicki Minaj's Anaconda halftime show.

Boolue called home missing his girls. No one answered his landline, nor did Ingram pick up her cell which vibrated from her Sex Code purse that lay at the passenger door near the feet of her twin's Louis Vuitton sandals. She hadn't ridden in the Lexus since Valentine's Day. She was worried, but a bit excited. She and the twins enjoyed hearing Daddy's rumbling beats.

She missed his call repeatedly. Boolue paced the Staple Center's lobby.

He could tell old girl either knew him from somewhere or anticipated for him to approach her. She followed him seemingly. Each time he glanced her direction, her dark eyes melted over him following a hot girl's exotic smile.

Lil' Momma was hot. She was very much stuntin' in her Kardashian skirt and stilettos. Boolue stood there peeping baby fluttering her round eyes in details of his swag. He wore an iced out Goon ski mask medallion that hung from the platinum Diddy chain. She proceeded a sly grin followed by a wink. The woman cared less of seeing what he had expected of her. Home girl kneeled and flipped through a magazine from a bottom shelf revealing her silk thong that exotically marinated between her caramel apple bottom. She pretended to read slowly. She longed and waited for his husky voice. The exit door buzzer sounded. She stood and glanced over her left shoulder for him. He had vanished.

Boolue had returned to his seat with two drinks. The game had started into the mid third quarter. Steve Nash stood at the foul line shooting an 'And One'.

The Suns were on a 10-0 run.

Freddy-B slid to the edge of this seat barking at the refs for bad calls as Boolue strolled through his missed message for the exact time Ingram had called three hours later.

Suddenly, the smell of *Helena Rubinstein* by Demi Moore oozed from baby that had been following him. She was a mixed breed diva curved to death. Boolue and Freddy-B admired her beauty as she stood at Boolue's right knee holding a pen and pink sticky pad.

"Excuse me," she motioned hunching her slender bare shoulders with an innocent smile.

"Yeah, what's good, shawty?" Boolue murmured out as Freddy-B interrupted.

"Beautiful thing!" He embraced Boo's shoulder with much care. Freddy-B took a profound liking for Boolue though the youngsta was a cold, calculating killer, and evidently born with a map to a woman's sexual appetite and the Rude Boy loved it.

Another thing he admired about the kid was the realness in his spirit and that the workers gave him just as much respect as they once did Rude Boy Claud. The crucial part of it was that Boolue was told Freddy-B never called the hit on Paula's B-D Tearence. Claud lied! The hit was signed by him alone. Freddy-B gave no fuck who smoked Rook. To him Rook counted shoe money. The Lakers and Kobe heated up returning a 14-2 lead by the third quarter buzzer beater shot by none other than the Black Mumba.

"Isn't your name Boo Boo or something like that?" the woman's sweet lips asked.

Freddy-B stood to his feet leading the hysterical die hard Laker fans as Avant featuring KeKe Wyatt's, *Nothing In This World*, played over the loud speakers. Boolue glanced at the big screen then back into her cunning eyes.

"N'all baby. It's Boolue. What's your name?" he returned.

"Trina," she noted tightening her eyelids over her prescription filled hazel brown contacts, lightly tapping her Bic ballpoint pen onto the sticky pad browsing his name through her mental Rolodex.

Within seconds, the young graduate refreshed memory. "Oh, that's where it's from. I met you at my cousin's funeral last year in St. Louis."

He cornered his eyes at Freddy-B. Boolue was flabbergastedly moved to of heard someone from so far away mentioning Paula's fallen baby's father's name so freely. He rushed to his feet and led ole girl to the men's John to better assess her relations with Paula's lover. His analytical thoughts were settled after she confessed being the one who stood next to Paula that held her left hand in prayer at Tearence's funeral. Boolue could hardly recall it despite her information was on point.

Further they talked and admired each other's gaze. Trina placed her palms under his shirt and slid them over his bare chest. She yearned to be penetrated. Her cleavage swelled. The thought of being caught pushed her even closer to him. Trina had just turned 30. She was fully developed with no kids.

Her split was ripe, tight and ready to be bitten.

Boolue felt every motion of it as she pressed against his growing bone longing for her heated slit. He soully resisted cheating on his wifey, Ingram. The moment was filled with overpowering temptation. Trina smelled of *Sex Amannia* fragrance by Courtney Smith. Caught in the moment, they passionately kissed.

The warmth of his tongue filled the cool of her wet mouth in pleasure. Her clitoris throbbed in heavy pulses as Paula's Skype app vibrated Boolue's right hip pocket.

Babyface's, *Who's Gonna Love You*, now displayed over the Staple Center's loudspeakers. Boo pulled away from Trina's wet tongue probing his neck, and answered Paula's cell.

"Get at me," he answered.

Paula soaped between her thighs as she showered. "I got your email. Why are you in L.A. when the slaughter should of gone down months ago?" she whined.

"Well, that's kind of a long story, but don't trip. Yo dude's on point.

Our deal is sealed. We're on the last out and the pitcher is up to bat as we speak, yan ming," Boolue assured Paula's worries.

"Pop hitter, huh," Paula smiled under a low grunt as she kneeled to gather her fallen Vera Wang scented soap. The echo of tiny droppings of water danced from the tip of her six month pregnant belly striking a nerve in Boo's loins. Paula showered at the least moments. Carrying her load kept her creamy.

She hadn't had sex since old Scotty.

"Gotta cool mama off, huh," he teased as his bone lengthened harder at the thought of seeing Paula bare wetness covered in soap. Paula had grown much thicker. She still rocked the flyest gear. It was diva until she leaves this crazy green earth one day no time soon. So she thought.

Trina slowly massaged the tip of his full erection. He tightened his eyes closed in pleasure, "Damn, girl. You better stop." He pushed Trina's hand away.

Paula assumed he meant her. She frowned. "Not in yo' wildest dreams. You'll have better luck at a KKK sermon before you get some of this pussy, so cross yo' legs you freak."

He ignored her as she continued.

"You need to handle yo' business like yesterday. My baby will be in this world soon and you can trust she won't live having to look over her shoulders and neither will I. You got that?" Paula barked.

"That's pussy," Boolue agreed. Deep inside, he wanted to tell Paula the truth. He found new evidence that Freddy-B had nothing to do with killing her lover. He felt she would consider he'd grown soft and became afraid to complete the hit; the truth being untold. Claud was an out of control gofer of his first cousin Rook behind Freddy-B's back. Boolue knew when the diva spoke, her word was final.

"One, consider it taken care of tonight." Boolue had no idea he could have ended the bloody war at that moment. Paula was weakened despite her pregnancy. She had always internally pondered for a way out. She wanted to live as peacefully as her girlfriends. She was amazingly street smart and gifted with reading men. Paula had only a ninth grade Vashon High School education. She swore her baby girl would be the coolest, most beautiful and educated princess that ever walked under the moon she adored every night.

She thought the world of Jenna. Jenna was going to be born protected like Sasha Obama. The day she take her first breath would be the official divorce of the trillion cut assassin and the dope game forever. Everything was going amazingly swell in her life. Her, Linda, and Diamond formed an inseparable love bond filled with wealth and a sense of comfort which had finally embraced Paula's world. She had slowly begun cutting her ties to the game. She had planned to pass the torch to Uncle James while she escaped the U.S. with her family and mini fortune one day soon.

Matt had become her salt shaker at the club beside Tangy who gave the club conflict and spice. Tangy had once GoGo danced at the Doll House in Miami.

She also sold her share of pussy in nearly eleven states. Tangy's slutty swag grew on the girls fast. She taught them how to draw in hot celeb crowds and get that paper from them horny weirdoes and widower husbands without having to buckle down fucking every customer for extra cash. Her metaphor was that, 'if you don't get caught, it ain't cheating.'

Paula paid them double the amount of any stripper's salary. Her girls were clocking Vegas prices. She was very proud of Tangy for her skills.

Worm was later indicted on a cocaine conspiracy. No one knew it but Boolue.

The Fed's hauled him back and forth from the Federal Clayton County hold over and released him on the weekends as a C.I. (Confidential Informant).

He bothered not getting any legal assistance. It was said in the Fed's, an underpaid attorney held the same legal power as a P.D.

Gifted with being born half mixed, Worm's other half paid off in his favor. White always favored in court. His P.D. turned out to be an old flame his brother Matt was banging from high school. A white girl named Robin.

Shit was about to get real sticky.

CHAPTER TWENTY-ONE – Read 'um & Reap

After hours of flying from L.A. to the great city of New York, Boolue awoke early the next morning on high from the great time he'd spent with Trina. He 'Soprano like' flipped the lounging room's tan curtains open as if he ruled this city of dreams. The 87 degree sun rays warmed the marijuana scented suite fast.

Freddy-B rested in the master bedroom. The pilot and their driver slept next door and waited for their next flight instructions heading back to St. Louis. Relaxing on chill mode was over. It was time for business. Both men dressed in Mauri suits with matching square toe gators. Neither of them wore jewelry. Their meeting was scheduled next door to Frank Lannodo's Boutique on Hillside Avenue. The actual money and drug exchange was thought to be made twenty miles away in a remote metal crushing yard where Bullet planned to dispose of the Rude Boy. Usually, Freddy-B would make an exchange only accompanied by his armed driver, but Shit had changed.

Boolue was heavily armed with a shoulder held SR 556 Ruger in the trunk of the silver 2013 Mercedes E-Class he drove. Freddy-B had no clue Boo packed the heavy artillery. Although, both of them wore a bulletproof vest under their white button down shirts.

A school of pigeons scattered from the open dumpsters and rested on the rooftops as the men parked between a 2010 V8-1138 horsepower Corvette ZRI Rhino, blood red on chrome deuces 22" rims. On the left sat a '09 SRX Cadillac truck, stainless gray with

Baghdag temporary license plates beyond the 5% tint. The whole scene was out of routine. To the Bumba Clot Freddy-B, his brother Bullet was customary to high profile and classy living. Normally the price tag for his whips were at least 100 racks or better. He informed Boolue of it being odd they were low maintenance vehicles parked in Bullet's private parking.

Freddy-B insisted Boolue play the shadows and keep his keen eyes peeled for possible jack boys or the Feds.

Boolue called them by cell, who calmly sat one minute and 21 seconds away in a universal black GMC Terrain SUV on black factory rims. Boolue called the meet a no show. He suggested the driver fall back and relax at their room and not to answer any calls unless it came from his number. He then ordered him to park the SUV into the lower level garage after he prepped the pilot to leave soon. Boolue calculated his moves to burn them all during the transactions. The two men weren't searched as they entered the rear steel door.

Bullet's security escorted the men to their assigned tables.

Inside there were hidden surveillance cams surrounding them. The Jamaican staff catered to the high end customers that seated throughout the five star restaurant in numbers. To Boolue, it was as if every dish that the well dressed dark complicated dread wearing women and men served, smelled of gourmet.

Bullet and six others sat chatting with exotic foods and drinks in a private section. Two well trimmed Europeans, an Arabian black man and two Asians sat together. Bullet surprised Freddy-B being there was a number of seven men seated as the Rude Boy bowed into his seat in reunion with his crime brothers.

Boolue patiently seated in the place of the older chauffeur at a table just ear shy of the men. His service was on the house, unlimited. He never for a second removed his eyes from their corner table. The men continued their meeting for nearly an hour downing the best white wine and giving Mob affiliated handshakes and nods. It was one deal after another, it seemed.

Freddy-B's back faced Boolue. Bullet faced him. Between the two Jamaicans, Boolue had no idea which was the one Black Randy called Bullet. Randy had never seen him face-to-face before. He'd only listened to Claud tell his war stories about the Jamaican God.

As Boolue adjusted the band on his leather Cartier watch, two huge goons dressed as if they were Miami Vice dick boys dressed in black RocaWear open blazers stepping towards the VIP circle of seven headed off towards the kitchen after a smile and nod from whom Boo was now sure was Bullet doing most of the talking who everyone seemed to love and trust. The two men returned to the kitchen. Boolue focused his stare through the crack that parted the service door. He pretended to sip his drink and to have been watching an old school classic, *Kings of New York* from the sixty inch monitor hung over the crowded bar.

Boo noticed the two men handing one of the waitresses a platinum dinner platter on the other side of the double sided serving doors. The half nude woman hurried across the room with a smile and placed the platter at the center of the men's table. No one removed the shiny top.

Freddy-B was fingered by Bullet to leave the table. The two men got up and made their way to the front entrance and stood out front smoking cigarettes seeming to be embracing business. Boolue peeped the move. The Arabian gentleman removed the top from the tray. There lay a white hanky. It and whatever lay under it was pressed under the table to the other Rasta that frowned towards Freddy-B. The goon tucked it into his waist and rose from his seat.

By the time the other two goons looked around for Freddy-B's new driver, Boolue had vanished. The men sprinted through the kitchen. They searched for Boo. It was a hit. Boolue read it as if he was a wasted white whore at a bar with no panties on. They were about to be fucked. The goons reached the rear parking with their pistols drawn, pissed to have only found the trunk of Freddy-B's Mercedes hung open.

Bullet locked eyes with the ball face Jamaican exiting the front entrance in what seemed to have been filmed in slow motion. The hit man bolted his 44 Magnum at the Rude boy's head.

Bullet's eyes widened. The Bumba Clot read them. He quickly faced the gunman and covered his face with his forearms. He wasn't afraid of dying.

The Rude Boy shouted, "Bummba!" He yelled for Boolue's attention. Bullet crouched over. He ran as if he was dodging the loud crackles from the fiery barrel. The first two shots passed into Freddy-B's side before landing across his elbows and into the torso of his Teflon vest. The force from the impact violently toppled the Rude Boy, tossing him through the restaurant's patio glass table. The hit man's shots increased. Two others tore through his left knee as he squirmed in the fragments of scattered glass in great agony.

All Freddy-B could hear were the sounds of rapid motor vehicle horns blowing and the sound of bystanders as shoppers cried out in fear, trampling over one another, hiding behind parked cabs and mailboxes for coverage. Sirens echoed quickly from blocks away. He could hear a constant beat of falling bullet casings tumbling just near where the gunman stood.

Freddy-B's eyes remained glued shut. He only opened them at moments. The element of surprise shook him. He tugged at a sense of his own mortality.

Boolue sprinted from the restaurant's gangway just in time. The Rasta stood over Freddy-B.

Thunderous sounds muted the traffic and witnesses whisperings. The intoxicating sound of Boolue's SR 556 Ruger muffled Freddy-B's ears. The heavy artillery vibrated the tiny storefront and skyline office windows as the rugged metal tore Bullet's hit man a new ass. As the shells hit the pavement, literally you could see through the hit man's torso. Boolue melted a sequel of rounds far and abroad into the dead Jamaican's body and continued his fierce epilogue, turning his S.R. towards Bullet's crowded restaurant, waving a vicious spiral assault at the two goons that now charged toward him firing from their fully auto Mac 10 Uzis.

The foot soldiers were demounted in their tracks by Boolue's spray of fire.

"Rude Boy! Won come on mon!" Freddy-B whined tearfully.

Blood ran from Boolue's nostrils due to the tragedy of the shattered glass ricocheting into his face. He helped the injured crime boss onto his feet.

Bullet hid out in a clothing store calling his army,

Freddy-B knew Bullet had to leave this form before he'd ever rest again.

He knew just about where Bullet hid himself. The men scuffled through the trails of the gangway. Boolue literally drug his boss to the awaiting Mercedes where he tail spun away from the small lot. Boolue quickly headed back to the hotel. The Bumba Clot ordered Boo to double back to finish his now sworn enemy.

Boolue refused. "Man, are you crazy?" Boolue shouted. "I got the pilot on standby. We gettin' the fuck out of New York!" He harshly argued. Boo had closed the curtain on the scene behind him.

The great Jaguar sneered and crumbled his fist into Boo's collar. "Me soul said, turn diss ting around! Dim already dead!" He spoke of the pilot and driver, knowing if Bullet planned to hit him, that he'd also made their death reservations. It was the hit game in full swing.

What the Rude Boy failed to know was that Boo had the driver to leave Freddy- B's 7.5 mil in the hidden compartment of the truck not far away. Boolue raced back towards the hit site. Freddy-B had now lost a lot of blood.

He painfully pointed out a Dutchness shop. "Him soul in dare! Me want him dead," said the great Jaguar as saliva popped from his lips. His eyes widened as if he'd seen a ghost.

Boolue said, "Fuck it! This fool may be looking for me next."

He unseated the Mercedes with his SR in hand wearing a Gucci hanky drawn around his nose as he stormed through the small boutique. Everyone who stood quickly hit the deck. His eyes searched wildly in sequence for signs of Bullet. He followed the frightened employees. They would definitely lead him to his target. He was right. He slammed his foot into the light wooden door suddenly behind the last woman that entered. Bullet's rugged voice came to him as he stepped over the threshold of the door. Bullet cowered.

He grabbed one of the ladies as a shield by knife point. Sirens closed in just down the street.

A single unit NYPD patrol car arrived at the scene. Backed up traffic hid the double parked Mercedes. The officer radioed for back up as he entered the gun smoke infested restaurant. Bodies lay scattered in blood, as some begged for the Officer's help. The customers and employees who weren't injured hid under the cherry wood tables.

Boolue extinguished three rounds through the lady's pale soft skin, killing them both. Her body slumped over the Jamaicans. He coughed in thick blood.

Boo crouched his weapon over his shoulder making his escape simple and unrecognizable.

Bullet wheezed out the final moments of life. 'So this is what hell looks like,' he thought as the light of hell covered his awareness, nearing his death bed. As he faded, his eyelids glued shut.

As they pulled away, Freddy-B boldly yelled out in his native language.

Boolue had no idea what Freddy-B had said. It was time he got the fuck out of the city of Satan.

The Rude Boy's words meant, "He was Queen's new God."

Bullet's heroin cartel connections in Kingston only spoke in dead presidents and bodies. In Kingston legal pharmaceutical companies lengthened their establishment through a wall of corrupt government officials, and hired Jamaicans and U.S. Coast Guards. They were unstoppable.

Freddy-B planned to soon buy first hand from them. The Rude Boy suggested there were no need for them to return to the hotel. The driver lay by the door, the pilot lay face down execution style beside the trampled table where he had sat playing solitaire, the playboy bunny marked cards scattered around in his blood. "Noon-God Blood!"

Both men's throats had been slit after they'd taken several hot ones to the back of their domes. The room was trashed and Boolue's rose gold jewelry was taken by the hit men.

Freddy-B needed immediate medical care. Boolue rushed down Vanwyak Expressway Freddy-B consumed the rest of Boolue's vodka to ease his chronic pain. Boo used his GPS to guide him to a Jamaican hospital emergency entrance. Freddy- B was dropped off and said to of been a victim of a carjacking two blocks away. Boolue lied to the authorities.

On Hillside Avenue, there were many car dealerships. Boo searched them for new transportation. He walked to the nearest Ford dealership and copped a Tina Marie white with black guts 2/10 Ford

Taurus.

After the NYPD questioned the restaurant's employees, an APB was issued on the silver Mercedes. Boolue tucked the Benz in between a blue Yukon and a Warner Brother's minivan that sat on a Dot's shopping mall lot.

Boo immediately phoned home.

Ingram's voice mail once again picked up. He was even more pissed. It wasn't the time or place for her mad wife home alone vindictive games. He needed her on some real talk. Faced with little to no time, he had to call Paula for her to Western Union him a few stacks as a down payment for the car.

He needed an anonymous SOS and name as well to clear the loan process.

She snapped, "What the hell are you up there doing?"

He filled her in on point. Paula pondered the details. She assessed her own arrangement. She done as he asked from Tangy's portable laptop.

Boo stayed at Lacy's, a sleazy motel, for two days. He only left once to check his trap back in Queens at the casino hotel. He tipped the valet to enter the garage. The money was still there as he planned. He FedEx'd the 40 inch Sony T.V. monitor filled with the money to his granny's house for safekeeping and returned to the hospital.

A day and a half later, Freddy-B was released. The Bomba Clot Rude Boy was admitted to a wheelchair. Boolue played his role well.

He visited Freddy- B for two hours each days he was hospitalized.

The men returned to Hustle City. Freddy-B was too weak to handle his business. He was forced by his private care giver to remain on bed rest. Boolue was sent out the second they arrived to collect every dime the Rude Boy workers possessed.

"Fuck this nigga and that bitch!" Boolue argued to himself. He had a loving family to attend to. He rushed down 70 West toward home.

On arrival at his destination, the unthinkable vindicated his heart of what he feared the most. Settled dried blood stains appeared from his bedroom to the basement door. It was as if a body had been dragged.

He screamed out, "no! No!"

He then repeated to call each of their names holding his 40 Glock as if a detective searching a dope house for a wanted fugitive gazing beyond the threshold of his basement. It was more than he could bear. Sitting on the custom theater recliner was his Beau Ingram's snuffed body. Her legs lay bulged open. Her unshaved vagina hairs engulfed the batting end of a baseball bat shoved deep inside her. Boolue ran to his Queen's body. His first intent was to pull the bat from its gripping end out of her. "It may hurt her!"

He empathically thought fast, embracing her head and shoulders paraphrasing in mind. "Who did it, where is my twins and how could I have been so foolish and money savvy to stay away from my family leaving them so unprotected?" he cried out and apologized to her corpse as he rocked her stiffness back and forth.

The playful image of his girls threaded his thoughts in pain. He sprinted to the open patio door. As he stepped foot onto it, he called out for them again by their nicknames.

"Lexy! Lan-Lan!" The worried father frantically searched the pool and garage area. There was no sign of them. The driven father looked towards the girl's life size Queen Sasha's play castle. Frightenly there was huge blood stained handprints covering the small castle's drawbridge door handle. Veins popped from Boo's forehead. He could hardly breathe. It was something no mental training could prepare a man for. He drooled from his mouth. His nose ran.

He reached for the door, but found not the strength to face what lay behind it. Unfortunately, he had to find out.

He held the handle of his gun onto his forehead anxiously shattered. On his gutsy pull, the small door fell at his created Rec. Boots. Miraculously, the girl's small bodies lay side by side. They'd been hog tied and were unconscious. They weren't injured.

Bullet, like *Tony Montana* had a heart for children, unlike Freddy-B. The goons sent by Bullet had been ordered not to execute the children.

Boolue was blessed with the fortune he had always fathomed since he was a poor child, window shopping and most of all, his babies were still on this earth with him.

You know what they say, 'All the riches in the world couldn't compare to a love you once knew'. Ingram wasn't coming back, he knew that much. This had to be Boolue's turning point for the sake of his beautiful girls though their mother was gone and somehow Freddy-

B honored the fact Boo saved his life back in Queens. Therefore, he'd granted Boolue's wishes by respecting his bow from the game. It was too late for Freddy-B himself. His soul was marked for death in Queens by the remaining six of his circle of trust.

He was that one case, where they say, "you can't teach an old dog new tricks."

His Rude Boy family was all he had to live for. He was in up to his nappy, sweaty nut sack; the opposite for Boolue's situation.

Freddy-B's biological seeds were survived by him. Sadly that he never returned to view the bodies of his wife and siblings whom were a sure sign that death awaited around the corner for him. Boolue prepared to fight Ingram's mother and father for his parental rights back.

◆

Luckily for Boo, Worm was detained by the DEA and Cape Town, Missouri ATF's task force for a case that spawned from a few petty hustlers born to envy other niggaz in the game clocking major dollars. His sudden arrest stemmed from gossip handed off to the DA that led back to an old case Worm caught before he met Paula. Worm's creepy half-hip ass faced fifty years. They threw the book at him. He literally pissed down his leg. He did what most pollenized niggaz do after they find themselves cornered in that small room handcuffed across from them Dick Boys breathing down their necks twisting the truth claiming to throw the book at 'em. Worm told everything he knew of Paula's drug ring and a few bodies she had her word wrapped up in that brought her Boot Hill operation problems over turf. It was whatever with whoever when it came down to Paula eliminating their native

240

competition throughout Missouri, which only led to her being picked up one star studded night by the DEA on Scotty and Linda's fifteenth anniversary that he had no idea even after their ugly expensive divorce Linda still celebrated with the girls at Paula's newly remodeled club, The Wet Diamond.

♦

April 02, 2014, Friday Afternoon

Eighteen months seemed like an eternity to Paula. Approximately 3:34 P.M. downtown St. Louis, AKA Hustle City, where cool rain drizzles zig zagged the 16th floor window of the United States District Court for the Eastern District of Missouri.

"All Rise! The Honorable Judge J. Shaw residing over case #9-91988A, UNITED STATES VS PAULA K. ROBERTS, AKA China," Marshal Big Will shouted.

The courts reviewed a new juror on the behalf of Ms. Roberts' request after an exhausting seven months of ongoing discrepancies and snarls over witty looks from jurors six and twelve. In a case of a drug cartel, murder, money laundering and racketeering sat before Paula choking the little life she'd accomplished since everything she ever loved was taken away. A young, figurative attorney, Ms. Eva Pace, was hired at Paula's defense through a Las Vegas law firm. The attorney was said to have been an associate of Tangy's father. Paula had literally taken Tangy from Worm's busta ass. After Tangy finally stood up to him, she fled to Paula with a fractured foot and minor skull injuries. She never returned to him.

Paula had winged her amongst her dangers at the club. Something

Tangy loved doing other than being out in them sticks under Worm.

Paula dared Worm to come within a thousand feet of any of her girls again.

"That Coop would handle his ass if he done so."

Tangy's father was an Alderman of St. Louis' Kintlock County. On this day,

Ms. Pace wore one out of her Infinity selection of breathtaking DGB double breasted skimpy skirts from her walk in closet. It was time for her to raise the bar. Paula was running out of ground in her case. The attorney was blessed with a back ground which allowed her the eye to see through the bullshit in the criminal system. Therefore, she would go to bat for people as far as the crooked law allowed her.

She was fortunate to have walked away with a law degree, although her gutta street sense fathered her social acceptance around her colleagues. They were too Booshie for her. She worked alone.

Four of the twelve jurors were older, bi-racial men and elderly white school teachers which turned out favorable in the Government's defiance. Those crooks played the race card with her by stacking the deck with tons of what they called ghost dope and twisted witnesses. They say God works in mysterious ways.

The newly appointed jurors were more of Paula's peers. They themselves were middle aged black men, who had suffered also the pains of poverty in Kintlock County. Tangy showed her ass this time. Paula smirked.

The juror six and twelve drooled behind Ms. Pace's class, swag and stunning curvaceous 36C-38-40 striking frame as she requested a short recess.

"Granted. Court is adjourned until Tuesday, 7:15 A.M.," Judge Shaw ordered.

The members of the court's staff cleared quickly. Attorney Pace remained standing, shifting through a stack of scattered files over the black wooden desk. Paula was escorted out in cuffs by sheriffs to a small urine smelling barred cell where she sat considering why and who were the government's so called C.I. they held two floors up as the smoking gun against her. None of her guys would crack. She pondered giving all she knew of their life long criminal histories.

Ms. Pace went over the CI's testimony. It was critical. Her client's soulful swearing convinced her that she'd never once had the guts to kill. She couldn't fathom a woman so beautiful and silent being an assassin as the prosecution described her client being a female monster.

Paula lied. "I never done business outside of account receiving for Diamond at the strip club." Paula claimed her extras came from the night shifts done over time, private dances.

Eva recalled the entire trial was an act of the white man trying to destroy another black woman. She was wrong.

Paula refused to lie down and let those mother fuckers curse her mother's legacy without them killing her first. After all, she'd fucked, bled, cried and put up with Peter's lousy ass throughout the sickening dreading days of her young life. She prayed in the name of Farrakan,

Obama, T.D. Jakes, and Monique. It didn't matter at this point. All she knew was that she needed a physical god to deal with this physical devil.

For minutes on, Jenna, Paula's twenty one month old daughter sat in her Uncle James' lap, too young to understand why her mother had been gone bye bye for the last year of her life. And why was she always bound up in those chains like her Shitzu puppy be when her uncle took them walking through Forest Park. Her eyes never left her mommie's presence.

James said nothing; he sat there sizing up the evidence, edging to figure out which one of those bitch niggas out there done crossed his niece. Judging the look on little Jenna's face, seeming as if she thought the same as he.

Besides, Paula had ordered her baby girl not to attend her high media trial.

She felt it would expose Jenna's identity. Her uncle J. brought his niece despite her falling wishes knowing each of Paula's court dates could be the last of his niece. He knew all too well how raw those white folks play the game when you had that bread they couldn't tax. Especially when it comes to inner city blacks. He also believed Jenna seeing her own flesh and blood stand ten toes down through a Loss,- Loss situation would gift her someday with the wisdom to conquer the next chapter of her journey in taking on her mother's empire. Uncle James knew Ms. China wouldn't fold. She had been raised with respect for the game.

"Die with honor," he always told her. Uncle never lied to Jenna.

As so Paula, since she too was much younger. Despite the smoking testimony from the C.I., he had to of been prepped by the prosecution due to the findings. The witness stated elements that proceeded during the time Paula was in St. (Ginnervie's) Federal custody revealing information that only could've been leaked from the F.B.I.'s investigation files. In which contradicted the so called arresting officer's written complaint. Meanwhile, ten minutes before court was set to continue, Ms. Pace reminded herself of the 1.5 mill cash and death threat Coop imposed behind Uncle James' knowledge. Even better, Eva's firm was paid $60K from Paula's strip club account from Diamond's laptop.

The prosecution smelled roses at the win of their case. Mrs. Tunnel's hand clutched a fist pump as the jurors, Paula and the News 2 team crowded like Payparazzi into the pine scented courtroom, excited just to get a glimpse at Hustle City's most feared boss bitch since the days of Tia and her $2.7 Mill prostitution ring.

Meanwhile, Paula's people were in position to buy out the Roberts Brother's entire real estate holdings. They owned Mid-U-City.

Everyone orderly formed a silence. The marshal's wore tan khaki pants and shirts with dark brown lines down their sleeves. They carried forty Glocks, hand cuffs and mace around their black holsters. Each of them stood as if ready to fire. Being that court was set to begin within the next few minutes.

It's been said, "Every rose has a thorn to protect itself." so Attorney Eva Skyes sat boggled in mind, based on the allegations of her client. This case was do-or-die.

Coop made the bashful attorney feel as if her very own life stood before the peers of the courts. The young attorney seized the moment to gut the Worm and stick it to those Federal Fuck boys like gumbo. The 1.5 mill Eva would earn stood her to retire with ease, and return to Jersey with her sister Lawanda.

Ms. Sykes excused herself from Paula's presence carrying a black folder under her left armpit heading to the bullpen where the C.I. sat being briefed by the prosecution. The C.I. was 5'11" blonde caucasian woman wearing light brown rectangular shaped Michael Kors glasses, rocking an all black knee high Liz Claiborne pin-striped and double breasted jacket, with the most amazingly smooth legs wrapped in waist high leggings. Her smile and cunning southern voice was an oily thief, believable, twisted full of lies and wicked. Eva hid behind a vending machine at the end of the short hallway, jotting down Ms. Tunnel's foolishness word for word.

At this point, all the mysteries had unfolded and made complete sense to the wise attorney. Worm and other so called C.I.'s were indeed coerced to create false accusations against Paula. Her devious paid attorney stood there thinking, "Paula would definitely be acquitted and the prosecution would gladly kiss my round black ass in exchange for my silence." Her pen paused.

The rapid clicks of Micro Tip pumps approaching fast. The platinum eyed bleached blond proceeded past Eva and spoke dumbfounded, startled to see her standing at the small microwave looking to be heating coffee from a Styrofoam cup.

Eva responded white girlishly, "nothing bitch," she whispered.

246

The prosecutor continued her way down the quiet hallway literally peeking over her narrow shoulders, curious of just how much of her conversation did the attorney actually pick up judging the look in Eva's eyes. Ms. Tunnel's face turned towards the sound of Eva's phone vibrating at her hip. Eva turned her back speaking into the tiny receiver.

"Hello, what's up girl?" she whispered.

"Bitch, you won't believe what Balenda is out here doing on the side of this house again."

Eva had previously warned her about turning tricks around their spot. For that dope, Balenda gave no fuck where it went down as long as afterwards, she had that glass dick in her mouth.

Balenda was Tam's mother. Tam continued, "Swear we moving off this west side away from her ass ASAP! She not finna keep making these niggas look at us like we some hoes, too."

"Bitch, you is!" Eva teased.

They laughed.

"Tam, I'll hit chu back on my next break. Can't talk right now. Shit is all over the place in this building today honey," said Eva.

"Bitch, why you whispering? Sounding all syfy and shit?" Tam chuckled.

Eva spoke through her teeth, "I'm in a fucking court session. Bye, crazy."

Tam lowered her voice. She knew her friend well. "Hoe, who you finna squeeze info from?" she asked.

Being the ole girl was out of sight, Eva cleared her voice and proceeded to shatter the Government's star witness. Risking her job wasn't important. Her neck was on the chopping block. A bitch had to grow some balls fast.

Little did Paula know, Coop would have slapped the peppermint taste out of her mouth and flexed the butt of his ratchet at her as he stood in her office handing her a personal five thousand in cash to let her know it wasn't a fuckin' game.

"I got this rat by the tail," Eva grinned.

"Ooh, yo' ass scandalous! You gone get cho red ass fired bitch. Keep playing games with them white folks shit."

Eva paused outside of the C.I.'s cell. She twisted her heavy glossed lips at Tam's sassy comment.

"Now you know they don't like yo' black aggressive ass anyway," Tam hurled as she stretched across her queen bed. Her soft Vera painted toes pressed against her headboard as her middle fingers molested her sticky creamy clitoris, fantasizing of how sexy Eva looked slithering out of her gear after a long day at the office. It was always hard for Tam to keep her hormones in check around Eva. She guessed it was more of the thought of her desire for thick women and the fact Eva was her best friend and ever so strictly dickly.

And not to think they shared the same showers and undressed girl friendly which always of been an instant cum for Tam. Just as the one she was enjoying as they spoke.

Eva's Rhihanna accent raved arrogantly. "Well, until they figure a way how to nail me, I'm keeping this size six stiletto on these crooked bastards necks with a smile like Trina," she laughed.

Tam fell silent in heavy, slow asthmatic breaths and restricted moans leaking onto her dark blue silk sheets in thick cum.

"Bi crazy!" said Eva.

Eva made her way into the open bullpen and executed her plan to the fullest.

Worm was relieved there wasn't a chance he'd see daylight again without having to be exposed in trial as Paula's C.I. He knew the consequence which came with being a rat. In short breaths, the theory of his fate changed.

Eva's testimony revealed as a true revelation for him. She then ran down in details of his bogus deal with the government. She assured him that she had means of clearing him from the Fed's 851 enhancement or else she'd nail his ass alone with those dirty fuckin' federales. She promised him either way he saw it, she'd win at the end of the day though she was more than grateful to walk out of that courtroom every afternoon alive, well and free, not worrying about having a 256 lb celly strip naked in front of her every night or some Arabian Nation Brotherhood whistling across the rec yard to have her carved like an ice statue with a homemade ice pick.

Eva's penitentiary spill shattered every thorough bone in Worm's body.

Not that any were ever there. Regardless of his decision, he was walking a green mile the moment he stepped foot into that courtroom. Staring down the barrel of Coop's forty was the last place he wanted to be heading. The look on his face showed clearly that he was going to cooperate to the fullest extent that he possibly could, which sat deep into his face like death as Tunell stood before him and the D&G smelled attorney. She had doubled back finding herself standing behind Eva's virtuoso frame with blushed brown eyes.

"Ms. Pace! What in the hell are you doing questioning my witness?"

Eva boldly faced her. "I'll let you figure that one out, Mrs. Tunnell. Goodbye, see you in court." Eva noted glancing at her Lindsay Lohan watch returning to greet Paula with the good news.

Friday, August 13th, Paula walked out of the United States Federal Building not guilty.

Pleased with the outcome of her dreadful situation, although Trayvon had lost, one of us had beat them dick suckas! She noted as she slowly stepped her neon stilettos into a platinum Regal driven by Coop.

Losing everything she owned throughout the course of her hateful trial was worth the news she received as she faced the front page of the evening Whirl Paper Coop handed her. It was the resurrection of the last pain that covered her past. Tone and his brother BowDidley were assassinated in an open and closed case where the blood brothers bodies were found beheaded in an abandoned downtown East St. Louis apartment of the Johnny Shields Projects. Where detectives discovered two ounces of China White heroin in the residence, Homicide Detectives told reporters.

Paula's eyes tightened vindictively with a pleased smirk at a job well done by Lil Jimmy. It was more than a blessing to know her enemies now rested in piss! Not to mention the warmth that filled her heart to have her life back and to put her club in safe keeping with her two untouchable bitches, Diamond and Linda, who waited with a surprise party at the strip joint with Paula's mother Pam.

Pam's case was up before the Supreme Court and over turned as temporary insanity.

Suddenly, Paula's mobile hook came alive. It was Worm informing her that he had the remaining of her twelve stacks. He was wired. She agreed to meet him later. She prepared a special black shirt, stat boots and Uncle James' throwaway red Beam State Trooper's forty Glock for the special occasion with the rat she loved to feed six hot ones.

Within hours later

Coop pulled onto Paula's club white and pink gravel stone parking lot. Her eyes narrowed carefully scanning her new dancers, anxious to sit them hoes straight on how the boss bitch Ms. China gets down vs. Linda and Diamond's settled ways.

She was ten times as hungry for that paper now after losing a nice portion of her powder coke that she had Linda hand off to James for him to drop the bricks on O.G. Prued Ell from St. Louis' Southside Grape Hill Crip Gang. In which, he sent word back to James that Tank and L-Dog formed the Sick Gang had gotten into some beef with

Tarowbei and Dre from Dub Street Crips and the eleven kilos got jammed up between a few murders that went down on Park Avenue. He lied and kept the work shaking on Grape Hill.

That was a mission Paula was prepared to deal with later. Her main concern was the cash she spent buying back her freedom. It was a breath taking moment for her to finally be able to take her princess to Disney World and collect her paper that nigga's thought they got away with.

She was even more excited to slide into some real gear and her open toed six inch electric blue Zyion Gadaz vs those nay blue wide leg smelly St. Jennivy County Jail jumpsuits and bright orange flip flops she wasn't about to get used to. She observed how adorable Tam looked in her new outfit.

Tam had really cleaned her act up with a grown and classy flavor. Paula smiled as Coop proceeded to open her door. Apple bottom asses swallowing new variety colored thongs crowded the two-door Eighty-Six Regal.

The girls' faces were filled with tears of relief to see Paula back home well and ready to continue her control of the streets. Linda and Diamond had each of them working less hours and no one was thereby allowed to pick up a single bill from the stage after hours, Lonna and Platinum tried Linda's hand once and resulted with a Colombian dragging across the gravel parking lot from Linda, Diamond and Tam. Nor were the girls allowed to be caught having sex with any of the customers anymore during business hours. The club had fell under strict protocol due to Paula's trial being so ugly and them people stayed lurking looking forward to finding any speck of illegal activity popping off that linked to Paula's involvement where it would justify stripping Diamond and Linda's established accounts business license and have them on trial as well.

As Paula's heels hit the gravel, open arms and hands covered her. The new girls joined also that they had heard so much about her being everyone's lifeline for so long. Cameras and Apple phone lights flashed and sparkled from Coop's rose gold diamond Cartier watch as he tightly gripped at her elbow leading her into the club's mirror tinted ten foot tall doors.

Paula literally fell to her knees after she entered and saw the joint covered in celebration decorations. At her surprise, her mother Pam stood there beside Linda followed by tears and inviting hands of Diamond tossing big face hundreds towards her. Uncle James chilled in the cut on point. He promised never to lose her again.

He blamed himself for Paula's troubles. He swore another motherfucker wouldn't live long enough to think about crossing his niece ever again. Paula collapsed into her mother's arms as her teary eyes read over the welcome home card Pam placed into her hands.

Dear Pauli,

I know time has passed and at many times the world and its evil tried to destroy our promise that we'll be together again and live life to its fullest for Carla, but this moment is evidence that our love is stronger than those who wished to tear us apart. And speaking of that baby girl, Scotty was extradited to Cuba last week and released yesterday. I left him with the information of that Boolue fella for him to handle. Yeah, look forward to reading about him too.

Welcome home Ms. Lady,

Mamma Pam

VOLUME II

October 28, 2015 Paula breached the delightfulness of her Phoenix Arizona eighteen story Latin Girls Escort Service office around five fifteen, after a long flight from visiting home in St. Louis, celebrating the Cardinals game seven World Series Championship. She sat at her glass desk over viewing the city of Phoenix waiting for Coop to return from retrieving the package. She was more than excited to be finally putting her eyes on the back burner of her past ties to the streets of Hustle City, anticipating seeing the head of the Don Dada of the once treacherous Rude Boy crime mob.

Paula howled at the sight of her Uncle James head that tumbled over her tiny toes as the box slipped from Coop's grasp. Paula gasped to take in what air stood between them.

It was more than losing a friend and an uncle. James had a heart of gold for his people. Coop upped his ratchet staring over the mounted digital photo of Scotty, Linda, Diamond and Paula out at the Black Essence Awards for Linda's B-day.

"Not ma fuckin' uncle, no! James, don't leave me!" She cried trampling into Coop's arms covering her eyes into his Prada shirt as he dialed out to Linda's cell wondering what in the fuck was going on. That Scotty's hit man had sent James' head instead of Freddy-B?

They swore blood behind the hit.

"Coop, we're at war with the Colombians. Scotty's a dead man," Paula promised.

Previously

Santiago, a made man from Scotty's cartel connect, mistook the white Bentley James drove of being Freddy-B's white maserati Turismo, leaving game six of the World Series Game where Santiago met the white car at a stop light on Broadway and Washington Street downtown St. Louis at around 10:51pm.

The black '07 Aston Martin slid up behind James undetected. James was wasted from the last hours of the evening celebrating the home team's win loving the taste of his Hennessey mixed drink AKA Incredible Hulk and the stadium's classic Budweiser beer. He sat patiently at the light carefree leaning with his forty Glock covering his lap. He'd gained his license to carry. James hadn't been high in eighteen months now.

As the dark window lowered, James flinched for his burner misfiring it from the sudden jerk. An arsenal of mini fourteen bullets carved into James' windows and door panels just as the gunman pulled beside him.

James' whip smashed into a movie DVD Red Box outside of Walgreens. Santiago then ordered his passenger to decapitate the marked man's head and bring it to him where he later that morning ate breakfast and mailed the unknown head to the address Scotty gave him.

TO BE CONTINUED!

THE DIAMOND ASSASIN VOLUME II

COMING SOON!

Contact yo boy at FAME0813@gmail.com

Author: FAME

Love Always,
Mother: Couretha Smith
Grandmother: Naomi Carte